Reclusive

Portrait of a Woman
Book 4

Kari Lee Harmon

OLIVERHEBERBOOKS

Cover art by Dar Albert at Wicked Smart Designs

Published by Oliver-Heber Books

0 9 8 7 6 5 4 3 2 1

This book is dedicated to all the women who are shy, awkward, self-conscious, and uncomfortable in social settings. It's not easy to put yourself out there, but sometimes the most magical things happen when you do. Don't ever be afraid to be you.

A special shout out to my fabulous editor, Alaina, who makes me look better than I am!

A heartfelt thank you to my amazing publisher, Tanya, who continues to believe in me and works harder than anyone I know!

Chapter One

re·clu·sive

ADJECTIVE

Seeking solitude: retiring from society

The late June day was gloomy as spring faded away and summer began. My father, Mortimer Smith, stood out back of our funeral home in our yard that faced Freedom Lake. He was dressed in his Sunday-best black suit in front of Father O'Dority, with Sister Mary Agnes standing witness. I stood beside my father as his best man, in a black-and-white suit that looked more like a prisoner's uniform, while his fiancé's sister was a no-show in her duties as maid of honor.

I looked behind us, but all the seats were empty.

No one had shown up.

My father, who was in his mid-sixties, had just

completed treatment for prostate cancer. He wiped the sweat from his brow, still on hormones and experiencing hot flashes. He shoved a black hankie back into his jacket then pressed a small device in his pocket.

Chopin's Funeral March started booming loudly from somewhere.

Glancing up, I frowned.

Since when did we add speakers to the funeral home's roof?

Thirty-five-year-old Samantha stepped out of the walk-out basement from the morgue, wearing her platinum blonde hair four inches high on her head. Her voluptuous body was encased in black silk, wrapped around her like a mummy, with a black veil over her smokey, painted eyes that were trained on my father like a zombie as she strutted down the aisle with determination.

"Dearly departed," the priest began.

I looked around the empty yard with a raised eyebrow. I was more comfortable with the dead than the living, but I wasn't sure even they had attended.

"We are gathered here today in the sight of those who have crossed over, and in the presence of anyone crazy enough to witness this solemn union of Mortimer Smith and Samantha ... er, well, Samantha in unholy bondage."

The priest didn't know her last name any more than I did.

Wait ... did he just say *unholy bondage?*

"If anyone can show just cause why they should not be joined, speak now or forever hold your complaining."

I opened my mouth ...

My father gave me a pleading, sweaty look as he fanned his face.

Samantha NoName gave me a death glare as she swung her ball and chain bouquet.

My words froze in my throat as I contemplated what to do.

My father was old enough to be her father, which I couldn't seem to get past. My mother had died while giving birth to me, and he had never remarried. It had always just been him and me against the world. I was terrified for that to change. What if Samantha was only using him for his money? What if she hurt him?

What if they had a baby before me?

I blinked.

What was that sound?

It sounded like a whistle, far off in the distance. An engine was churning away, getting louder by the second. It didn't sound like a car or truck or boat. I looked up. The sky was darkening, but I didn't see any airplanes. The roar of the engine boomed louder than the thunder that rumbled overhead.

Lightning zipped across the ominous sky, and we all jumped.

A big fat raindrop fell on my cheek, as if even the Heavens didn't approve of this union.

I lifted a hand and wiped the drop away as I looked at my father helplessly.

"This is all your fault, Morticia. Why can't you just be

happy for me?" My father looked at me with such disappointment.

"I want you to be happy, Dad, but—"

"Yeah, no one is here because of you. Why do you have to be so creepy?" Samantha pouted. "All I wanted was to be your new mama, honey. What did I ever do to you that was so bad? Why do you hate me?"

Mama? I mentally rolled my eyes. "I don't hate you, Samantha."

She sniffled. "She won't even call me Mama. Make her go away, Mortimer. She's ruining our union."

"Seriously?" I gave up trying to be nice.

"This wedding has become a funeral, I'm afraid," Father O'Dority said grimly, sending a disapproving look in my direction.

Sister Mary Agnes furiously worked her rosary beads, her bugged-out eyes gaping behind us. "We're all doomed because of her." She thrust a finger in my direction. "The mistress of death."

"You're all crazy." I shook my head. What the hell was happening here?

A loud crash sounded behind us, and we all whipped around and screamed. As if in slow motion, a train came barreling through the funeral home, headed right for us. Mayflower had a train? Where were the tracks?

We were all going to die ...

That was the last thought I had before I closed my eyes in anticipation.

I screamed again when loud booms startled me, and I

fell off my bed. Prying my eyes open, I looked around and realized I was in my bedroom. The boom sounded again, and I breathed a sigh of relief. Someone was knocking on the door to my apartment. I blinked as my words sank in.

My apartment above *Smith's Funeral Home.*

I ran to my window facing the backyard and lake. The grass was still intact and the house still standing. Thank God I'd been dreaming ... more like having a nightmare.

"Morti, are you going to open the door for me or not?" a male voice snapped with irritation.

I slipped a robe on and hurried to open the door. My father stood on the other side of the threshold, looking tired and stressed and more than a little frustrated.

"Dad, you're okay." I threw my arms around him.

"Are you?" he ground out.

I stepped back at the tone of his voice. "Yes," I frowned over his narrowed, annoyed eyes, "why?"

"You were supposed to be at work an hour ago." He pulled out a handkerchief and wiped his damp forehead. "These damn hormones are worse than the prostate cancer."

"Oh, shoot." I winced, *so* not ready for menopause and hot flashes. "Sorry about both." I ran to get dressed. I never overslept.

"*You're* sorry?" He grunted from out in the living room. "You don't have to deal with Samantha in planning this wedding. Your mother and I eloped, but Samantha wants the whole kit and kaboodle." He sighed. "This wedding is going to kill me yet."

"Then maybe you shouldn't get married?" I tried one last time, biting my bottom lip as I emerged from my bathroom, dressed and ready to go.

He scowled. "For the last time, Morti, this wedding is happening. You're supposed to be my best man. It would be nice if you started acting like it." He turned around and left without another word, and it suddenly dawned on me ... no wonder I'd had a nightmare.

My *life* was a literal trainwreck.

LATER THAT NIGHT after an insanely busy day at work, since my father was MIA as usual, I was finally home. I showered, leaving my wet, waist-length black hair down to dry, and slipped on my dark gray, sensible cotton t-shirt and matching pants set, even though summer had begun. I didn't like my legs touching when I slept.

Skin-on-skin made me clammy.

I shuddered just thinking about it as I grabbed a pint of Rocky Road ice cream and a glass of milk because, hello, the road I was about to travel as *best man* in my father's wedding to a child was definitely going to be rocky.

I carried my treasures to my gray sofa and took a moment to appreciate my clean, white, minimalist apartment. White, gray, and black made me feel at peace. Too many colors made me anxious. And the only decorations I had were books by my favorite thriller author, Oliver King, taking up any available space.

I had read every book in his *The Shadow Files* series and seen every movie adaptation. One of the biggest streaming platforms had even just picked up the series to be adapted to a TV show. I couldn't wait to binge-watch every episode once the show dropped.

Pushing the newest book, *Behind the Mask*, aside to make room for my laptop, I propped my bare feet on my coffee table and logged into *The King's Quills*, an online chatroom fan page for lovers of all things Oliver King.

Mentally and physically exhausted, I had no time to date. Not to mention, I was socially awkward with people in person, especially men. The only way I had ever made it on the cheer team back in high school was because I had three best friends supporting me every step of the way.

Zoe, Tiffany, and Harmony still did to this day.

Other than them and our weekly girls' nights at each other's houses, I didn't need anything else except maybe a diet cola. I liked being alone. It had always been just my father and me. When I got old enough, he converted the upstairs of our funeral home into two apartments, so I could have some independence.

My new Mommy Dearest had already insisted he move in with her, so I was more alone than ever. With my work schedule and spending time with my best friends, I had little time for anything else. Online dating satisfied my need for intimacy, while cybersex and a good vibrator took care of everything else. The problem was ...

I wanted a baby.

I was nervous about giving birth because of my mother's experience, but I was allergic to animals, so having a pet for a companion was out. I just really wanted something of my own to love and be loved unconditionally. I knew I could adopt, but a part of me wanted a baby of my own. Someone who was like me genetically, who might actually *get* what it was like to be me. I knew it was selfish, but if Mommy Dearest had a baby before me, I would seriously lose my mind.

My screen lit up with a fountain pen avatar that made me smile.

Collin Quinn was in the room.

He had been a member of the group as long as I had. We were both superfans of Oliver King, often debating who was the bigger fan, much to the amusement of the other members. There were hundreds of members in our group who lurked, but only a handful of us diehard fans were active. The rest loved to watch and learn. We were even talking about hosting watch parties when the show dropped, but we hadn't worked all the details out yet.

Oliver King had never been seen before, and no one knew where he lived.

He took his privacy seriously, so the people who created his fan page suggested we all use an avatar in his honor. No pictures. My avatar was a shiny star on account of my alias, Sybil Starr. I wasn't sure how many people used an alias. I simply did because it was more exciting for me to pretend to be someone else. Someone sexy. Someone wild. Someone carefree...

Someone I would never be in person.

I didn't know how I came up with Sybil Starr. It was just there in my mind, so I ran with it and never gave it a second thought. Everyone knew I wrote poetry, but no one knew I secretly wrote fan fiction. Oliver King hated fan fiction, because he believed his work was perfect as-is. I had to agree for the most part.

It was pretty hard to argue with perfection.

But in his later works, he'd incorporated a romance thread. Most likely because sex sells, but I found that aspect of the books lacking. So that was the part I loved to secretly rewrite. I didn't tell the group because of how Oliver King felt about fan fiction, but I was curious how others felt about the romance addition.

I picked up my laptop and typed a question in the chatroom.

Sybil Starr: *What do you think of the romance in Behind the Mask, Collin?*

Collin Quinn: *I don't. I prefer to focus on the thriller aspect of the novels.*

Collin seemed a little older than me, like maybe fifty. Over the years, I'd learned a bit about all the active members. He was a travel writer, working on a piece about small towns in America and unique aspects they're known for. He was a serious sort, but not afraid to speak his mind in his own blunt way when it came to the great Oliver King.

She Wolf: *I think everything Oliver King touches turns to gold. He's brilliant.*

She Wolf's avatar was a wolf. She never gave us her

real name, but she seemed young, like maybe thirty. She did say she was a wildlife conservationist, and it was clear she was obsessed with all of King's books.

Hans Brewmeister: *Not everything. His last movie was a flop.*

She Wolf: *It was not a flop, but any poor reviews have nothing to do with King. That has to do with the people who wrote the adaptation. Movies are never as good as the books, in my opinion.*

Collin Quinn: *Agreed.*

Hans Brewmeister: *Well, I'm with Starr. I think the romance sucks. His writing is definitely going downhill.*

Hans's avatar was a mug of beer. He also seemed a little older than me, like in his fifties as well, and he did tell us one time that he owned a craft beer brewery. He was also not afraid to point out the flaws of Oliver King when something displeased him.

Sybil Starr: *I never said the romance sucks, and King's writing is as stellar as ever, but his heart doesn't seem to be in the romance aspect.*

Collin Quinn: *Maybe it wasn't his idea to add that aspect, Starr. Ever think of that?*

Tie Dye Dotty: *That's true. I wouldn't be surprised if his editor pushed for the addition. If you ask me, King can be a bit intense with his words. Maybe he needs a little romance in his own life. Peace and love rule the world, baby.*

Dotty's avatar was a Scooby Doo Van with pot leaves on the sides. She was admittedly a free-spirited, retired, hippie widow in her seventies, who loved the adventure of Oliver King's books.

Captain Rogers: *Well, now, there's a woman after my own heart. I'll sail off into the sunset to rule the world with you anytime, Dotty, just say when.*

Captain Rogers' avatar was an anchor. He was a retired navy captain who owned his own luxury yacht and chartered guests around for the fun of it. An admitted scallywag, he read King's books for ideas for the murder mystery dinners he hosted. Rogers had been sweet on Dotty for a while and kept trying to get her to go on an adventure with him.

Tie Dye Dotty: *You really are a scallywag, Captain.*

Stacy Rose: *Well, I personally love Detective Gideon Wolfe and genius reporter Serena Blackwood. I pretend to be Serena in every book.*

Stacy's avatar was a flower. She was in her forties, based on the fact that she'd been married for twenty-five years and married young. She was an at-home mom and homemaker who seemed really sweet and always had a positive attitude. If we met in person, we would be friends.

Marky Mouse: *I'm with Stacy. I like the chemistry between the two, and I like that King made her smart. She holds her own against him and sees things in his cases that even he misses, and he's not afraid to give her credit where credit is due. That's cool.*

Marky's avatar was a mouse, of course. He, too, was middle-aged, but he was single. He was a cheesemaker who ran his family's dairy farm in Vermont. He liked to read King novels to unwind, and was open to anyone who wanted to start a private chat, clearly looking for his own smart lady.

I often wondered if anyone ever took him up on that.

Suddenly, I got a notification that someone had private-messaged me. I set my empty Rocky Road container on my coffee table, my stomach churning in knots. My finger hovered over the private chat button as I secretly prayed it wasn't Marky Mouse.

I clicked on the button and blinked.

Collin Quinn.

We had an intense relationship. We would argue over different points of view regarding Oliver King's work because we were both passionate about the topic and always strove to be right. Then the next minute we would flirt. I could never quite figure out his hot-and-cold personality, but I had always been intrigued.

This was the first time he had private-messaged me, though.

Collin Quinn: *Hey, stranger, haven't seen you in cyberspace in a while.*

Sybil Starr: *Hey yourself. Been busy.*

Collin Quinn: *Writing poetry?*

Sybil Starr: *Among other things. You been traveling much?*

Collin Quinn: *Some. I'm running out of small towns to research.*

Sybil Starr: *I know all about small towns. Mayflower's the worst.*

Collin Quinn: *Mayflower? Connecticut, right?*

Sybil Starr: *Massachusetts.*

Crap!

I always strove to remain anonymous. It was fun to be free. I could say and do anything I wanted without fear of judgement. The minute I was Morticia Smith, men were no longer interested in me. I wasn't the uninhibited sexy Sybil Starr anymore. I was just plain ol' boring Morti.

I stared at the blank screen, wondering if he was still there.

Collin Quinn: *Guess I have another small town to visit.*

Sybil Starr: *Wait, you're coming to Mayflower, Massachusetts?*

Collin Quinn: *I don't see why not. I need more material for my research, and I finally get to meet the infamous Sybil Starr.*

Sybil Starr: *I don't think that's such a good idea.*

Collin Quinn: *It's happening, Starr.*

Sybil Starr: *When?*

Collin Quinn: *When you least expect it.*

Sybil Starr: *I don't like surprises, Quinn.*

Collin Quinn: *Consider it a plot twist.*

And just like that, he left the private chat.

Conversation over.

What would Collin do when he came to town and found out Sybil didn't exist?

Something clicked in the far recesses of my brain. Oh my God ... Sybil Starr did exist. I suddenly remembered where I had heard the name. She was a girl I went to high school with, who had moved away after graduation to become an adult entertainer with a stage name of Sybil Starr ...

A trainwreck didn't begin to explain what my life was about to become.

Chapter Two

"I made a huge mistake," I said the next day.

It was my turn to host our weekly girls' night in my apartment above my family's funeral home. I was too stressed out to go with a grand theme for food and drinks, so I just pulled together a hodge podge of items I had left over in my fridge.

"Oh, really? I hadn't noticed, doll." Tiffany Eisenhower-McGinnis eyed the half-eaten mac-n-cheese, baked beans, and meatloaf with wide eyes, as she raised golden blonde eyebrows over her periwinkle-blue eyes and pasted on a smile that showed all her teeth. She sipped her dry martini, shaken not stirred.

Tiff was engaged to Matthew McSteamy McGinnis, our big, strapping, curly-blond-haired local Irish pub owner, with charming baby-blue eyes and dimples to die for. They had adorable five-month-old twins. She ran a spa where she taught sensual massage for a living, but didn't have to work at all if she didn't want to. Her late Grammy had left her a fortune after she passed away.

She missed the grandmother who had raised her, but she was embracing getting to know her parents and twin sister, now that she was forty and had finally forgiven them for giving her away.

She was the one in our group who always encouraged us to keep going no matter what.

"You should have called, hon." Zoe Robinson-Anderson looked at me with sympathy in her amber eyes as she flipped her long caramel locks over her shoulder and poured herself a glass of Chardonnay. "I would have gladly come over early to help you with anything you might need."

Zoe was also happily married to our very own sandy-haired, hazel-eyed Dr. Hunkarama, aka Chaz Anderson, with the whisky-smooth voice. Zoe had turned forty-first in our friend group. After twenty years of marriage, her husband left her and their four children to find himself by backpacking across America. Zoe had picked up the pieces of her life and started her own party-planning business. Chaz went to high school with us and was four years younger, but he was happy to raise Zoe's children as his own.

She was the one in our group who always hugged us when we were down.

"Listen, babe, clearly something is up with you. So, spill it. How did you make a huge mistake?" Harmony

Jones raised pale-green cat eyes at me and shook her head, her red spiked hair not moving an inch. She popped the top to a beer, and proceeded to order a pizza and wings on her phone to be delivered.

Harm had just turned forty, and had met her life partner, Byron Studmuffin Storm, a honey-eyed, ponytail-wearing, mental health therapist with as many piercings and tattoos as her. He specialized in sex addiction. After a scandal forced her to go to SAA, even though she wasn't actually an addict, he became her sponsor, as a favor to the judge. Sparks flew right from the start, causing all sorts of trouble. Harm ran a new-age shop and dabbled in witchcraft for fun, not claiming to be an actual witch. He lived in Boston, and she lived in Mayflower, but they were making it work. They had only just begun dating as an official couple.

She was the one who always kept things real for us.

I adored and loved them all and didn't know what I would do without them. "You know that online book club I told you all about?"

They nodded.

"Well, it's a chatroom for fans of Oliver King."

"Isn't he that thriller author you're obsessed with?" Tiff sipped her martini, but didn't touch the food.

"Yes, and so is everyone else in the group."

"Well, at least you'll meet someone with the same interests as you, so that's good." Zoe nodded encouragingly.

"It would be, except ... I used an alias."

They all blinked.

"Why?" Harm quirked a brow at me.

"Oliver King likes his privacy, so no one knows what he looks like. We all use avatars for our pictures in honor of him. Some people use their real names, and some use an alias." I shrugged. "I used an alias, because I was afraid if I was my normal self, then no one would like me?"

"Oh, doll, how could anyone not love you? You're so smart and funny, and you have no idea how beautiful you actually are." Tiff squeezed my hand.

"I'm awkward." I sighed.

Harm grunted. "Dude, you're talking to the queen of sticking-my-foot-in-my-mouth. I was lucky Byron found me charming, when most men considered me a freak."

"Yes, but at least you speak. I clam up and no words come out when I'm talking to a man I'm interested in. Hell, I do it when talking to the living, period."

"You just haven't found the right man yet." Zoe patted my shoulder.

"Except ... maybe I have." I bit my bottom lip.

"Shut the casket!" Harmony gaped at me. "Seriously?"

"Um, details please." Tiffany popped the olive from her drink into her mouth.

"His name is Collin Quinn."

"Ohhh, I like him already." Zoe clapped her hands.

"He's a travel writer, researching small towns across America from unique angles."

"Sounds interesting." Harmony took a swig of her beer, looking off pensively.

I thought about that and realized I'd been intrigued by Collin Quinn for a while now. I had just never realized he might actually feel the same way, until our private chat. "He is. We've been in the same fan group from the beginning. He actually thinks he's a bigger Oliver King superfan than me, if you can believe it."

Harm barked out a laugh. "As if."

"Exactly. Anyway, half the time we're arguing points about King's latest book, and the other half we're flirting. At least I think it's flirting."

"Good for you for putting yourself out there." Zoe's tone held pride, as if we were her children.

I hated to let her down. "Except, I didn't really."

"What do you mean?" Zoe's brow quirked.

"Well, I used an alias, remember?"

"Oh yeah." Harm nodded. "Well, it's online, so how is that a problem?"

"Because he's coming to Mayflower."

They all squealed.

"What? When? We have so much to do to get ready." Tiff was already reaching for a notebook and pen.

"I have no clue," I admitted. "He said 'when I least expect it.'"

"Oh, my goodness, this is so exciting." Zoe grabbed her day timer.

"No, it's terrifying. He threw me off when he slid into my DMs. I didn't mean to tell him where I lived. I have no clue where he lives."

"A cyber relationship isn't nearly as satisfying as an in-person one, doll." Tiffany's tone gentled.

"Except I'm not who I said I was." I groaned. "He doesn't even know what I look like, and I can't use the alias I chose."

"I don't understand?" Zoe shook her head.

I paused a beat before I dropped the bomb, revealing how stupid I was. "Because I picked Sybil Starr as my name."

All three women gaped at me as obvious recognition dawned. How was it they remembered who Sybil Starr was immediately, and it had taken me so long to figure out?

Harmony's jaw fell open. "Um, dude, didn't the girl we went to high school with, Sylvia Stallone, change her name to Sybil Starr when she went into the adult entertainer business?" She stared at me as if she couldn't wrap her head around why I would want to use the name of an adult entertainer.

"Yes," I grudgingly admitted.

"Babe, what were you thinking in choosing that name?"

"I didn't do it on purpose. It just popped into my head, and I couldn't remember where I had heard it from. I also never thought I would meet any of these people in person. He's going to come to town looking for Sybil, but she won't be here. Everyone in town will tell him she moved away years ago."

"Wait, all is not lost. That's not a bad thing," Tiff

pointed out logically. "Then you can get to know him as yourself. And if there's not a spark, he'll be none the wiser and you can move on. Sounds like a win-win to me."

"That's true," Harm added. "He could be a troll, for all you know."

"Love is blind, ladies," Zoe added her two cents. "It doesn't matter what he looks like. I think it's wonderful that you connected without knowing what each other looks like. Beauty on the inside is far more important than external looks."

"But looks sure don't hurt." Harm laughed.

"Very true," Zoe added, "but many times someone you might not have noticed at first becomes beautiful on the outside after you get to know their personalities."

Tiffany nodded. "And many princes turn into frogs when you get to know their ugly insides."

"With my luck, he won't even show, so I really don't know what I'm worried about." The doorbell rang, and I breathed a sigh of relief. "Pizza's here." I ran to the door, hoping that was the last we would hear about Collin Quinn.

A WEEK later I was in the Mayflower library, looking up police procedure for a piece of fan fiction I was writing about Oliver King's latest book, *Behind the Mask*. Detective Gideon Wolfe was a brilliant investigator, but reporter

Serena Blackwood was an actual genius. King had them arguing over police procedure for a case he was working, which led to a sex scene.

Don't get me wrong, the sex was great!

I shivered, remembering the detail King had put into that scene.

It was downright delicious, but the motivation was off. It was almost as if someone had told him he needed to add a sex scene, so he just dumped one in without giving it much thought. Sex was about so much more than the physical act. I wanted to feel their emotions. See what was going on in their heads and not just with their bodies. I was invested in these characters, and he wasn't doing them justice.

So, I decided to change the scene.

I glanced around, making sure I was alone, as if someone could read my thoughts. I felt my cheeks flush hot. It wasn't like I was doing anything illegal, and it certainly wasn't like Oliver King would ever find out.

"There you are!" came a voice from behind me, and I jumped.

Whirling around, I looked at Samantha ... er, well, just Samantha. I really did need to find out her last name without coming across as a jerk because I didn't remember it. I pasted on a smile, trying to be nice, like I promised my father.

"Here I am."

"Shhhhhhh." Rose Theodore, Mayflower's librarian, held an arthritic finger up to her lips and gave us a glare.

She was a stickler for the rules. She didn't like anything outside the norm, like when Harmony kept books in her new-age shop. Books that Rose would ban, no doubt. And she certainly wouldn't approve of my fan faction, desecrating the work of a literary god.

"Are you avoiding me?" Samantha lowered her sultry voice, pulling me from my thoughts. She crossed her arms over her voluptuous body, encased in a body-hugging daisy-print sundress, and tapped her sandals on the floor in time with the second hand on the clock.

She was tall with long golden extensions. I didn't get it. She didn't look anything like my mother. What was my father thinking? My father was sixty-five and she was only thirty-five. I would be forty in a few weeks.

My father must be having a senior moment.

I just hoped he would come to his senses before he signed on the dotted line. "Of course I'm not avoiding you." I squirmed in my black leisure suit and gray blouse one size too big, tapping my own sensible loafers.

I hated anything tight that might reveal my shape. It made me feel like no one was looking at my eyes, like they didn't take me seriously. I had been humiliated by one too many boys back in high school. They only wanted me for my body. No one had ever wanted me for my personality. Ever since we graduated high school, I started wearing conservative clothes and my hair in a tight bun at the nape of my neck.

Sensible and tidy, just like me.

"Then why haven't you returned my calls or text

messages?" She narrowed her color-contact enhanced lilac eyes at me.

"I'm not on my phone much." I shrugged. "Guess I didn't see them."

"You could try a little harder, you know." She pouted. "For your father's sake, at least. He really doesn't need the added stress."

My heart sped up. "Why? Did he have a setback?"

"No, no, nothing like that. It's just the hormones are making him, well, hormonal. He cries over everything, and you're not helping by not being there for him."

"He has you now." I hated not being number one in my father's eyes anymore. "I didn't think he needed me, other than to run the funeral home."

Her voice softened. "He needs you more than you know. This wedding is a lot for him to handle."

I threw my hands in the air. "Then why are you planning such a big one if it's upsetting to him?"

She thrust her chin up, and her spine stiffened. "Because it's my wedding, too. He's not upset about the wedding details." She jabbed a long, manicured fingernail in my direction. "He's upset about you not being on board with this."

As much as I hated to admit it, she was right. I was being selfish. If this was what my father wanted, then I had to let him do it, even if I thought he was making the biggest mistake of his life.

I dropped my hands to my sides, my shoulders slumping slightly. "Fine. I'll try to do better."

"Don't try ... just do." She spun on her toe and sashayed her way out the library door, colliding with a man who was entering.

The man frowned and grabbed her arm to steady her. "Might want to look where you're going before someone gets hurt."

She huffed. "Well, that was rude."

"Not rude, just stating the facts, ma'am." He nodded once to her and then his eyes locked onto mine as she stormed out.

My heart fluttered, and I was unable to speak or look away.

He wore black jeans over black snakeskin boots and a black, collared, short-sleeved shirt. His hair was black as well and slicked back with silver at the temples. The lines and angles of his face were rigid and sharp, his stormy gray eyes intense behind a cool pair of round glasses that covered the longest eyelashes I had ever seen. Full lips were spotlighted in the center of a sleek, salt and pepper mustache and goatee.

He arched a brow when I just stood there like a dimwit, staring at him with my mouth open. He tilted his head and then stepped around me as he headed over to the circulation desk where Rose sat. I watched him walk, his gait smooth and stealth like.

"Can I help you, sir?" Rose tucked her pen behind her ear and squinted up at him.

"Yes. I'm new to town. Do you happen to know if there is a woman who goes by Sybil Starr that lives here?"

I sucked in a sharp breath ...

Collin Quinn was in Mayflower.

He shot me one final odd glance, and I pretended to choke on my gum as I mentally said every prayer I could remember from my youth to no avail. He was no troll ...

And I was royally screwed.

Chapter Three

I was exhausted, trying to avoid a certain travel writer for days. For a recluse like me, it shouldn't be difficult to avoid someone, but Collin Quinn seemed to be everywhere. I hadn't even gotten online because I didn't want him to ask me if that was my real name. I'd heard through the grapevine that he was staying at the *Mayflower Inn* and asking everyone about Sybil Starr. I would be mortified if he found out I had been pretending to be her for years.

It was July first. A new month. My birthday month.

Hopefully forty would be a fabulous year and not another forgetful one. I walked through the doors of *McGinny's Pub* and looked around, spotting Matt and Tiffany and Chaz and Zoe. It looked like Byron and Harmony weren't here yet. Heading in their direction, I felt like a seventh wheel for the first time. There had always been at least two of us who were single ... until now.

Everyone, even my own father, was happily partnered up except me.

These days it was a struggle to leave my house, especially with my work being right below my apartment. And now that my father had moved out of his apartment right next to mine upstairs, the house was eerily quiet.

The pub was busy as usual. Matt's cousin, Aidan, manned the bar, and his other cousin, Finn, played guitar and sang Irish ballads in the corner, with Tiffany's twin sister, Tabatha, front and center. Another happy successful couple. It really gave me a complex, and I began to wonder what was wrong with me.

Other than being a socially awkward recluse with a morbid sense of humor, that is.

"Hey, Morti." Zoe waved. "We haven't seen you in days. Where have you been, hon?" She sat all snuggled up to her husband, Chaz, securely tucked beneath his arm. They were going on four four-and-a-half months of wedded bliss and were happier than ever.

"Working." *And hiding.* "Dad's MIA again with Samantha." I sighed.

I hadn't told the girls that I had seen Collin just the other day in Mayflower, because they would be all over me to introduce myself. I didn't know if I was ready for that. I was hoping he would leave once he knew Sybil wasn't here anymore.

"Aww, doll, I hate to see you working yourself to death. You need to live a little. It's your birthday month." Tiff looked up at her fiancé, Matt, as he handed her a bubbling glass of top-shelf champagne. She winked up at him and blew him a kiss, then he and Chaz went back to the bar for more drinks and appetizers for the table.

"And your wedding month." I tried to deflect the attention off me.

"I know. Matt's family will be here the week of the wedding and the week after, so we can take a honeymoon."

"Oh, yay." Zoe clapped her hands. "You deserve this, hon. We loved France when we went on ours. Where are you going to go for yours?"

"The twins will be almost seven months by then. Between Matt's family and mine, they should be okay. An Alaskan cruise is on Matt's bucket list, and July is the time to go. Besides, who wants tropical in the summer?"

"Very true. I heard the inside passage is stunning," Zoe said dreamily. "All the little towns you stop at are so quaint and picturesque. And the College Fjord and Glacier Bay are supposed to be breathtaking."

"Hey, babes, what did I miss?" Harmony sat down, her boyfriend Byron already halfway to the bar to join the men.

"Not much." I shrugged. "Just discussing Tiff's honeymoon plans to Alaska."

"Cool. A nice, rugged choice for Matthew McGinnis the legend. And I'm sure they have a fabulous spa for our lovely Queen Tiffany."

"They do indeed." Tiffany winked.

"So, dude, where have you been?" Harm looked at me suspiciously.

"Okay, okay, you caught me." I shook my head. "I've been in hiding."

Zoe blinked. "From whom?"

Tiff arched a brow. "Samantha?"

Harm pursed her lips. "Your dad?"

"All of the above," I admitted, then bit my bottom lip before adding, "and more."

"More?" they all asked at once.

I smoothed my hand over my bun and then my pant suit, making sure everything was in place before blurting, "Collin Quinn is in town."

"Oh, my Lord, since when? Did you talk to him? What did he say?" Zoe's questions came rapid fire, and I could already see the wheels spinning in her head. "We need a plan."

"Almost a week ago. No. Nothing. And no *we* don't," I responded firmly to their questions. I adored my girls, but they could be a bit *too* helpful at times.

"You *have* to talk to him, Morti." Harm frowned. "Or is he actually a troll?" She shrugged. "I mean, like Zoe said, if you have a connection with him, then who cares, right?" She leaned forward and waggled her eyebrows. "So do you?"

My head was spinning. "Do I what?"

"Have a connection with Collin Quinn."

"Yes. No. Maybe ... I don't know." I shook my head. "I couldn't even speak when I ran into him. I didn't know it was him until I heard him ask Rose if she knew if a woman who went by Sybil Starr was in town. Then I knew it had to be him, and he looks even better than I pictured. Tall, dark, and more mysteriously handsome than a man should have a right to be."

"Morticia Smith, why didn't you tell us?" Tiffany tapped her fingernail on the table.

"Because I knew you all would make me talk to him, and I know I will turn into a complete idiot in his presence like I always do around men. Cyber Sybil had the connection. In person Morti ... not so much."

"Well, you might not have a choice." Harmony's gaze was locked on the pub door. "Based on your description, I'm guessing that's him, babe."

We all turned to look.

My jaw unhinged.

"What is he doing here, and why is he with my father?" I had a bad feeling I wasn't going to like the answer to that.

"Oh, doll, you weren't kidding. Mr. Collin Quinn is literally the quintessential heartthrob of every woman's story." Tiffany tore her gaze away from the table they sat at to wink at me. "Nicely done, Morti."

"I haven't done anything." I started to sweat as I was on the verge of a major panic attack.

"Yet ... he certainly is a culinary delight." Zoe sighed.

"You chose him long before you met him, babe. Twenty bucks says you turn fantasy into reality before he leaves town."

"I'm in." Zoe nodded with a wince. "All our love lives have been wagered on. It's your turn, hon."

"Same." Tiff laughed. "Turnabout's fair play, doll."

"With Sybil gone, there's no reason for him to stay in Mayflower, so there's nothing to bet on," I said, as more of a reassurance for myself. No way could I focus on the funeral home and my father's wedding with the likes of Collin Quinn walking around town. "Besides, I don't even know what I would say to him if I managed to speak at all."

"Well, you better think of something." Harm jerked her head toward the other side of the room.

I blinked. "Oh, God, why is my father walking this way?" What if Collin had somehow found out I was Sybil? My gaze darted everywhere as I tried to find a place to hide.

Too late.

"Morti, there you are." My father mopped his head with a handkerchief. "I've been looking everywhere for you."

That was rich, considering he was the one who was always missing lately. I bit my tongue.

"Here I am. What's up, Dad?" I kept my eyes trained on my father, feeling my cheeks heat just knowing Collin was looking at me. I could feel his intense gaze burning clear into my soul. What I wouldn't give to hide behind my computer screen right now.

"I would like you to meet my new friend, Collin Quinn. Collin, this is my daughter, Morticia Smith."

Great. Now I had no choice but to look at Collin. My gaze met his stormy one. "Nice to officially meet you, Mr. Quinn."

My father looked between the two of us. "You know each other?"

"We ran into each other at the library the day I arrived." Collin's gaze never left mine. He seemed to be studying me, taking in every detail. Then again, he made a living doing research. "Morticia. That's an interesting name."

"That's my father for you." I shrugged, feeling so awkward under his scrutiny, and finally tearing my gaze away from his. "He's an interesting man. You can call me Morti."

"Only if you call me Collin." His tone sounded amused.

I lifted my chin a notch and met his gaze once more. "I heard you asking for Sybil Starr. We went to high school with her. She's not here, so I imagine you'll be leaving."

"Quite the contrary." My father beamed.

I frowned.

Collin explained, "I'm writing a piece about small towns across America for a travel magazine. Mayflower intrigues me. I'm looking for a unique angle."

"Well, good luck with that. It was nice meeting you." I faced the girls, turning my back on my father and Collin, hoping they would somehow disappear.

"Morticia Marigold Smith, don't be rude," my father scolded. "I told Collin you're a wiz with computers and online research, and that you would be happy to help him with whatever he might need."

"Why in Hades would you do that?" I blurted, then

pressed my lips together, mortified that Collin had heard. My gaze shot briefly to him, and I watched the corners of his mouth twitch as if he were fighting a smile, then I quickly looked away as my father dropped the bomb...

"Because he's your new neighbor."

THE NEXT DAY, after a sleepless night with the usual creaks and groans of our ancient funeral home no longer comforting, I headed downstairs to immerse myself in work. I was a licensed funeral director, just like my father, with the intent that I would one day take over the family business. I just hadn't thought that day would come so soon. He was retirement age; he just hadn't prepared me for when he planned to leave.

He just left.

He was the main point of contact for grieving families, arranging and overseeing all aspects of a funeral service. He also handled our pre-need sales as well. While I typically handled the paperwork, preparing obituaries, death certificates, permits, and scheduling. I had an assistant, Gertrude Stout, who managed our billing, helped coordinate with vendors like florists and cemeteries, as well as other general office duties. She was a godsend, and had been like a mother to me.

Eddy Bender was our embalmer. He was gifted in making the deceased look remarkably lifelike. His mortuary assistant, Annette Minx, was a big help in maintaining our facility. Clyde Wilcox was our crematory operator. Beatrice Baxter was a funeral attendant who mothered everyone, and Eli Grimsley drove the hearse with never so much as a bump. It was a small crew, but we all worked so well together.

I was the one who was having an issue.

I didn't do well with the living, so taking over my father's role as well as my own was proving to be a challenge. I was no good at sales, and downright awkward when it came to comforting grieving loved ones. I'd lost more than one customer due to my bedside manner. Go figure. What they saw as rude was really just me being socially awkward.

After a long and trying day, my staff left, one by one.

Gertrude poked her gray head into my office and looked at me with kind brown eyes. "Now, closing time is closing time, Morticia dear. You're going to work yourself to death if you keep up at this pace. Your father wouldn't want that, I'm sure."

"I'm not," I mumbled under my breath, but nothing got by Gertrude.

"He loves you, honey. You know that. He's just got a lot on his plate these days, trying to keep up with someone so young."

I wisely kept my mouth shut on that topic.

"Just promise me you'll leave soon." She patted my back, knowing I wasn't much of a hugger. I didn't like to be touched. "Don't make me worry about you, too. Go on upstairs and relax. Take a bath and read one of those books you love so much. Okay?"

I smiled at the woman who had been in my life for as long as I could remember, and was so thankful she had been like family to me. "I promise I won't be much longer. Now don't make me worry about *you*. Get home safe, and I'll see you tomorrow."

She left, looking tired but a little less worried.

I rubbed the back of my neck, my head aching. I was looking forward to letting my waist-length hair down. A bath and a good book actually sounded great right now. Gathering my things, I locked up and headed upstairs.

Opening my apartment door, I carried my workbag into the kitchen and dumped my things on the table, too tired to worry about putting anything away right now. I slid off my black suitcoat and untucked my gray blouse from my black trousers, as I kicked off my loafers and groaned over my aching feet. Lifting my hands, I reached behind my head to pull the pins from my hair when I froze.

Goosebumps peppered my flesh.

I knew every creak and groan this old house made, and the dearly departed didn't have footsteps. I dropped my hands and spun around with raised fists, preparing to do whatever necessary to defend myself.

I let out a little shriek. "W-What are you doing in my house?"

"Renting the apartment across the hall, remember?" Collin's hair was still slicked back, his goatee as meticulously maintained as ever and glasses still perched perfectly on his nose, but he'd changed out of his slacks and collared shirt into a pair of black joggers and dark gray t-shirt. His boots were off, revealing dark gray socks.

"Exactly. So why are you in *my* apartment?" I crossed my arms over my chest, feeling exposed even though I was *nearly* fully dressed, and my hair was still up.

"You left the door open." He stepped inside and walked around, looking at my things.

I gasped. "That doesn't give you the right to enter."

Ignoring my comment, he homed in on the end table by my couch. With long strides, he crossed the room before I could stop him. He picked up a book, and my breath hitched as his eyes met mine. "You read Oliver King?"

I swallowed hard. Crap. I hadn't meant for him to ever find out I was a fan of Oliver King. The last thing I needed was for him to put the pieces of the puzzle together and guess that I was Cyber Sybil. All I could do was nod.

"Me, too." His eyes narrowed as he looked closer at all my sticky notes with scribbles in between the pages of the book. "You take notes?"

I hurried over to him and snatched the book from his hands, feeling the heat rise up from my neck straight to my ears. "It's a little hobby of mine." I clutched the book to my chest. "Anyway, how can I help you, Mr. Quinn?"

"Collin, remember?"

"Right." I walked toward my door so he would get the hint and follow.

He defiantly stood his ground.

I inhaled a deep breath and counted to ten. "It's been a

long day. If you could enlighten me as to why you're here, that would be most appreciated." I strove for my father's patience and tone, figuring I needed the practice anyway.

"Of course. My apologies." He joined me by the door. "Has anyone ever told you that you're a fascinating study, Ms. Smith."

"Morti," I said absently, trying to shake the haze from my brain his heavenly cologne had caused. "I've been called many things, but *fascinating* isn't one of them." I cleared my throat. "I-Is that why you're here? Because you find me fascinating?"

"In a sense, yes." He towered over me, studying my face as he spoke. "You would make a great character in a book."

"Do you write books?"

"I write articles for a travel blog, but I read a lot." His stormy gaze studied the features of my face, lingering on my mouth for a moment before meeting my gaze once more. Do *you* write books?"

I resisted the urge to look away. "I write poetry."

"Ahh, but we both love to read thrillers, I see."

"I guess so."

A pause filled the air between us until things became unbearable.

I squirmed.

He blinked.

"Anyway, I just moved in, and thought I would take your father up on his suggestion that I ask you for help on Mayflower's history. He says you have more information on all things Mayflower than the library and historical society combined."

I shrugged. "I'm into research."

"Then I guess we have more than one thing in common. So, what do you say? Will you help me while I'm in town?"

"How long will that be?"

"I'm not sure. Until I'm finished with my article, I suppose. So, can I count on you?"

If it would speed things up and get him out of town, then I was game. "Sure. But I really am tired, so if there's nothing else ..."

He looked off as if thinking. "I guess that's it for now. Have a good evening." He started to cross the hall.

I grabbed my doorknob with shaking hands, ready to call it a night and end my misery.

"Oh, one more thing." He looked back at me.

I blew out a breath. "Yeah?"

"You should join the online fan page for Oliver King. It's called *The King's Quills*. I think you would get a lot out of it."

"I'll keep that in mind." I gave him a quick awkward wave and then promptly closed the door in his face, leaning back against it to keep from falling.

What the hell had I just gotten myself into?

Chapter Four

I sat on my couch with a diet cola and a bottle of antacids, staring at my laptop. Sybil Starr had quietly left the group the second Collin had arrived in town. I'd made sure of that. I couldn't keep pretending to be her, now that I realized she was a real person. It had been a week since he'd rented my father's fully furnished apartment. I'd thrown myself into work and avoided him as much as possible, even skipping the July Fourth celebration, claiming to have a summer cold.

He hadn't come over to my apartment since that fateful night, thank the Lord, but it was still just as nerve-wracking to know he was under the same roof.

Inhaling a deep breath, I decided to join *The King's Quills* as myself, aka Morticia Smith, with a coffin avatar.

I hesitated for a moment, my finger hovering over the "Join Group" button. What if Collin recognized my writing style? What if he somehow figured out that I was

Sybil and used to be a member of this very group? But I couldn't resist the pull of reconnecting with my old Oliver King fans, even if I had to be more guarded now and pretend to be someone new.

Taking a deep breath, I clicked "Join."

Almost immediately, a notification popped up that my request had been approved. I scrolled through the recent posts, feeling a pang of longing as I saw familiar usernames discussing the latest theories about King's upcoming book.

A new post caught my eye.

Collin Quinn: *Has anyone heard from Sybil Starr lately? She seems to have disappeared.*

My heart raced. Should I respond? Before I could decide, replies started flooding in.

She Wolf: *No, I haven't seen her post in a while. Hope everything is okay with her.*

Hans Brewmeister: *Maybe she finally realized how overrated King's books are and left the group.*

Collin Quinn: *Then why are you here, Hans?*

Hans Brewmeister: *I keep holding out hope they'll get better.*

Tie Dye Dotty: *Now, now, Hans. No need to be negative. I'm sure Sybil is just taking a little break. We all need some time away from screens now and then. Time to relax.*

Captain Rogers: *Aye, our Sybil is probably off on some grand adventure. She'll be back with tales to tell, mark my words.*

Stacy Rose: *I miss her insightful comments. The group isn't the same without her.*

Marky Mouse: *Hey, we have a new member. Welcome, Morticia Smith.*

I froze as I saw my name mentioned. This was my chance to introduce myself, but what should I say? My palms were sweaty as I hovered over the keyboard. Finally, I shook my hands and then started typing.

Morticia Smith: *Thank you for the warm welcome. I'm new to the group but a longtime Oliver King fan. Looking forward to discussing his books with fellow enthusiasts.*

I hit *send* before I could overthink it. Almost immediately, responses started coming in.

Tie Dye Dotty: *Welcome, Morticia. Love your avatar. Very fitting for an Oliver King fan.*

Captain Rogers: *Ahoy there, Morticia. Always glad to have a new shipmate aboard. What's your favorite King novel?*

Collin Quinn: *Welcome to the group, Morti. I'm glad to see you decided to join. I look forward to hearing your thoughts on King's work.*

My heart raced seeing Collin's name and knowing he was just beyond the hallway dividing our apartments.

Stacy Rose: *Wait. Morti? You two know each other?*

She Wolf: *Well, that's hardly fair. You two know what each other looks like. Isn't that like anti-King?*

Collin Quinn: *I confess. I went to meet Sybil, but she wasn't in town. I decided to stay and do research for my* article. *That's how I met Morti, but I haven't seen much of her since then.*

My head was spinning trying to keep up, so I just started typing.

Morticia Smith: *Thank you, everyone. I chose a casket because I'm a mortician, and yes, I too thought it was fitting for an Oliver King fan. All of King's books are amazing. Currently, I am enjoying Behind the Mask. I love how King delves deeper into Detective Wolfe's psyche in that one, but I'd have to say The Midnight Cipher is my favorite. The twists in that one kept me guessing until the very end. And finally, yes, Collin and I have met, and yes, I have been MIA with a summer cold, but I can't say we "know" each other.*

Collin Quinn: *You're my research assistant, so I would say we'll get to "know" each other quite well before I leave. Providing you stay healthy long enough.*

I blinked. What exactly did that mean?

Before I could ask, Collin logged off.

I stared at my laptop screen, my heart racing. What did Collin mean by getting to "know" each other quite well? And why did he emphasize my supposed illness? Did he suspect I was faking being sick to avoid him?

My fingers hovered over the keyboard, unsure how to respond. Before I could decide, more messages popped up.

Tie Dye Dotty: *Ooh, sounds like there might be a budding romance in our midst. How exciting.*

Captain Rogers: *Aye, the lady doth protest too*

much, methinks. There be sparks flying between these two landlubbers.

Hans Brewmeister: *Great, just what we need—more lovey-dovey nonsense distracting from actual book discussion.*

I felt my cheeks burning. This was exactly what I'd been afraid of. I quickly typed out a response.

Morticia Smith: *There's no romance. We barely know each other. I'm just helping him with research, that's all.*

A soft knock at my door made me jump. I signed off before anyone could comment any more, then I hesitated a moment. I bit my bottom lip. Maybe he would go away. The knock came again, and I sighed as I slowly made my way over to the door. Taking a deep breath, I opened it a crack.

Collin stood there, looking unfairly handsome in dark jeans and a fitted black t-shirt. "Evening, neighbor. I was hoping we could chat about that research you promised to help me with."

"Oh, um, sure," I stammered, reluctantly opening the door wider. "Come in."

He strode past me, his cologne wafting in his wake. I closed the door and turned to find him studying my bookshelves intently. "Quite the Oliver King collection you have here."

"Yes, well, I enjoy his work," I said, trying to keep my voice steady. I walked over to stand near him, but not too close. "What kind of research did you want to discuss?"

Collin turned to face me, his stormy eyes intense behind his glasses. "I'm particularly interested in the history of Mayflower. Your father mentioned there are some fascinating local legends and ghost stories associated with the town. I thought that might make for an intriguing angle for my article."

"Oh, of course." I nodded, relaxing slightly now that we were talking about safer topics. "Mayflower does have quite a rich history when it comes to the paranormal. There's the legend of the Widow's Walk, the haunting of the old lighthouse, the mysterious disappearances on Freedom Lake ..."

"Interesting," Collin murmured, his gaze never leaving my face.

I shifted uncomfortably. "So, um, where would you like to start?"

He smiled, the corners of his eyes crinkling. "Why don't we begin with the Widow's Walk legend? That sounds interesting."

"Okay." I nodded, moving to grab a notebook from my desk. "The legend goes back to the early 1800s. A sea captain's wife would walk along the roof of their house, watching for her husband's ship to return. One stormy night, she saw a ship on the horizon that looked like his. As she watched, the ship was dashed against the rocks and sank."

Collin leaned against my bookshelf, his arms crossed as he listened intently. "And what happened to the wife?"

"She was so distraught that she threw herself from the

roof. The house remains vacant to this day and has become somewhat of a tourist attraction."

"Can you take me there?"

I swallowed hard. "Like ... a date?"

He shrugged. "A research date. Is that a problem?"

"Not at all." I forced myself not to fidget. "The house is on the outskirts of town, so I'll just need a few days to prepare."

"Should I call you?" He pulled out his phone.

My lips tipped up slightly. "I'm pretty sure I know how to reach you, neighbor."

His gaze dropped to my mouth. "Fascinating."

I blinked. "What?"

"Your smile."

I blushed. "Everyone says I have a Mona Lisa smile. I don't share it often."

"Everyone's right." He kept staring. "I feel privileged you shared it with me. You should do so more often."

"So ... it's getting late. If there's nothing else, I'll be in touch when I'm ready."

He bowed his head slightly. "I'll be waiting." And then he walked out the door.

It was mid-July and my birthday.

Nearly a week had gone by before I was able to cover my schedule and gather information on the legend of the Widow's Walk. The day dawned sunny and hot. My hair was secured in its usual knot at the back of my head. I wore gray cargo shorts, a black cotton blouse, and sturdy hiking boots. The house was isolated along the coast and on the farthest edge of town. We had to drive and park at the bottom of a cliff, and then hike up a hill to get to the top. The property was falling down, so no one was allowed to enter, but the views from the yard looking over the cliff were stunning.

"You ready?" I asked, when Collin finally appeared out front of the funeral home.

"Absolutely." He wore black jeans, sturdy boots, a dark gray t-shirt, and carried a leather satchel.

"What's in the bag?"

"A camera, notebook, pens." He shrugged. "The usual writing and research paraphernalia." He looked around. "Where's your car?"

I pointed to the vehicle by the curb. "Right there."

One black eyebrow crept high. "Seriously?"

I looked at my old, weathered hearse and frowned. "What's wrong with Fester? He might be a little odd, but he has character."

Collin's lips quirked. "Nothing, if you're planning on hauling back a dead body. Should I be concerned?"

"Hey, you never know." I wagged my eyebrows mysteriously, enjoying myself. That hadn't happened in far too long. "I always keep the old vehicles when my father buys a new one for the company. It beats having a car payment."

"I repeat, you are one interesting woman, Morticia Smith."

I felt my cheeks flush at his comment. "Well, shall we get going?" I said, trying to change the subject.

We climbed into Fester, and I couldn't help but notice how Collin's long legs seemed cramped in the passenger seat. As I pulled away from the curb, an awkward silence fell between us.

"So," Collin finally said, "how long have you lived in Mayflower?"

"All my life," I replied, keeping my eyes on the road. "My family has run the funeral home for generations."

"Have you ever thought of leaving? Seeing the world?"

I shrugged. "I've thought about it, but Mayflower is home. Plus, someone has to keep the family business going."

"Hmm," Collin mused. "Sounds like quite a responsibility."

"It is," I admitted.

"So, how do you know Sybil?"

My hands tightened on the steering wheel, and my lips parted but nothing came out.

"Your father mentioned you knew her when I asked him about her," he said, by way of explanation.

I cleared my throat. "Oh, um, well ... we went to high school together. We weren't really friends. She moved away years ago to pursue other opportunities."

"I see," Collin said, his tone unreadable. "It's a shame I missed her. I was hoping to meet her while I was in town."

"Why's that?" I asked, trying to keep my voice casual.

He looked off pensively. "She was always such an

interesting presence in the online group. I was curious to meet her in person."

My stomach churned with guilt. "Well, maybe she'll come back to visit someday," I said lamely.

We lapsed into silence for the rest of the drive. When we reached the base of the cliff, I parked Fester, and we got out.

"It's quite a hike up," I warned. "Are you sure you're up for it?"

Collin's eyes gleamed with amusement behind his glasses. "I think I can manage. I'm not as old as I look, you know." He smoothed a hand over his salt-and-pepper goatee, the light shining off the silver at his temples in his otherwise jet-black, slicked-back hair.

He didn't look old ... he looked hot as hell.

I felt my cheeks flush. "I didn't mean to imply ... I just ..." I trailed off awkwardly.

He chuckled. "Relax, Morti. I'm teasing you. Lead the way."

We started up the steep path, the July sun beating down on us. I was grateful for my sturdy boots as we navigated the rocky terrain. Collin kept pace easily beside me, barely seeming winded.

"So, tell me more about this legend," he said as we climbed. "What happened after the wife threw herself from the roof?"

"Well, according to the story, her ghost still haunts the house," I explained. "People claim to see a woman in white pacing along the widow's walk at night, still searching for her husband's ship. Some say they've heard her wailing on stormy nights."

"Spooky," Collin murmured. "Have you ever seen or heard anything yourself?"

I shook my head. "No, I've never experienced anything supernatural in Mayflower, even with working and living in a funeral home."

We reached the top of the cliff, both of us slightly out of breath from the climb, me more so than him. The old house loomed before us, weathered and gray against the bright blue sky. Its widow's walk was clearly visible along the roofline. I led the way round the entire property, talking and pointing out photo ops as we walked.

"Quite a sight," Collin remarked, pulling out his camera to snap some photos.

I nodded, gazing out at the expansive ocean view from the edge of the cliff. "It's beautiful up here, isn't it? You can see why she would have spent so much time admiring the view and watching for ships."

"Indeed." Collin's camera went off one more time before he lowered it, staring at me instead of the horizon.

I blinked. "Well, this is it. We should probably head home. It's going to take a minute to climb back down and drive to town."

"Why in such a hurry? Am I keeping you from a date?" His eyes held a twinkle, but I could tell there was a seriousness lurking behind the humor.

"Something like that," I admitted.

"Oh?" The twinkle dimmed slightly, but I noticed.

"I have a date with my best friends," I admitted, not sure why I felt the need to clarify. "It's my fortieth birthday today."

"It's your birthday?" Collin's eyebrows shot up in surprise. "Why didn't you say anything?"

I shrugged, feeling uncomfortable under his intense gaze. "I don't really like to make a big deal out of it."

"Nonsense," he said, shaking his head. "Forty is a milestone. We should celebrate."

"Oh, that's not necessary," I protested weakly. "Really, I'm fine just having a quiet dinner with my friends."

Collin's mischievous gaze locked onto mine. "I can be quiet. Come on, let's head back to town. I have an idea."

Before I could object further, he was already heading down the path. I hurried to catch up, my mind whirling. What was he planning? I didn't like surprises.

Then why did the thought both terrify and excite me?

Chapter Five

The drive to town was filled with an anticipatory silence. I kept sneaking glances at him, trying to figure out what he was planning. He seemed lost in thought, a small smile playing at the corners of his mouth.

As we approached Lighthouse Lane, he finally spoke. "Take a right here."

I frowned. "But the funeral home is to the left."

"We're not going to the funeral home," he said mysteriously.

Curiosity got the better of me and I followed his directions. We ended up parked in front of *Pilgrim Perks Cafe*, the local coffee shop.

"Wait here," Collin instructed, before hopping out of Fester.

I waved to old man Truman Winters, who was headed in for coffee alone, and the guilt hit me hard. He was our mailman, who wore the thickest glasses and yet still mixed up our mail. Long past retirement age, no one cared, because it gave him a purpose since his wife passed away.

Zoe baked him pies weekly. Tiffany gave him a massage monthly. Harmony hooked him up with the best essential oils for healing. And I was his normal coffee date. I would have to make it up to him soon, but with my father MIA, I had very little time for myself.

I watched through the café window as Collin went inside and spoke animatedly with the barista. A few minutes later, he emerged carrying two large to-go cups and a small paper bag. Gerty and Gabby Rogers, our resident busybodies, whispered with their heads bent close together as they passed by Fester and pointed at Collin heading right for me. I could only imagine tomorrow's headlines in the Mayflower Gazette ...

Local Mortician up to Mischief with Mysterious Stranger!

Collin returned to the car, snapping my attention back to him as he handed me one of the cups and the bag. "Happy birthday," he said with a small smile.

I looked down at the cup, seeing my name written in neat cursive on the side. I couldn't help but smile back at him. "Thank you."

"Hot white chocolate with extra whipped cream," he said.

My lips parted. "How did you know?"

"Trade secrets." He winked, taking a sip from his own cup. "Americana for me. Now, let's go find a place to sit and enjoy our drinks."

"I know the perfect place." I drove for a few minutes, farther down Lighthouse Lane, and pulled into the park. We got out and sat in the gazebo.

"This is perfect," Collin said, and handed me the paper bag. "And here's your birthday treat."

I peeked inside to find a double-chocolate-chip muffin, my favorite indulgence. "More trade secrets?"

He shrugged. "I may have done some reconnaissance work while talking to your employees at the funeral home. I like to know who I'm dealing with before letting them drive away with me."

I laughed. "I'm hardly scary."

"You would be amazed at the seemingly innocent people I've met in my travels." He gave a mock shudder. "You're right, though. You're definitely tame by comparison."

"Or boring."

"Hardly."

"Well, thank you." It had been a long time since someone had gone out of their way to make my birthday special. Without my mother around, my father just didn't know how.

As we sipped our coffee and chatted about our lives, I found myself opening up more and more to Collin. There was something comforting about being around him, as if he truly understood me without judgment or pretense. Probably because he came here to meet Sybil, not me, so I could relax without romance involved. He told me a lot about himself as well, which I gathered wasn't the normal case. He seemed like a very private individual, just like me.

Before I knew it, it was getting late.

"We should probably head to the funeral home if I'm going to make it to dinner with my friends."

"By all means." He picked up our trash and threw it in the trashcan on the way to the hearse.

A few minutes later, I pulled into the parking lot of *Smith's Funeral Home* and parked out back. I locked Fester, and we headed to the door to our apartments.

"Thanks again for the birthday surprise. It was thoughtful and quiet and exactly my style." I graced him with another rare Mona Lisa smile. He'd earned it.

"You're welcome." He smiled back. "Consider it a thank-you for your help with my research."

"It was my pleasure." But I had to admit I was relieved that was over. Small talk was normally so hard for me. I liked my privacy, and I'd already revealed too much to him. Better to keep my distance before getting hurt.

"Good. Then you'll let me know when our next field trip is."

I blinked, but was saved from answering when the door burst open.

"Thank God you're back." My father panted, out of breath. He fanned his flushed face.

"Is something wrong?" I grabbed his arm, my heartrate speeding into overdrive.

"There's been an unexpected death in town." He glanced at Collin while he said that.

Collin looked at me and then at my father. "Should I be concerned?"

"On the contrary. I imagine you will be elated." My father's mouth stretched into the widest grin I had seen from him in a while.

I frowned. "Dad, why would anyone be happy about someone's death?"

My father shook his head. "Not happy about that. I mean, Dante Stallone died in a freak accident this morning, involving leftover fireworks from the Fourth. His niece, Sylvia, is his only known living relative. I had to call her this afternoon and let her know so she could make the proper arrangements."

I could feel my face pale.

"What exactly does that have to do with me, and why would that make me happy?" Collin's forehead puckered.

"Because Sylvia Stallone changed her name after graduation to Sybil Starr and then she left town," I said, in barely more than a whisper.

"That's right," my father nodded, adding, "It's your lucky day, Collin Quinn, because Sybil Starr is coming back to Mayflower."

I DIDN'T SEE Collin for the next two weeks.

As promised, Sybil Starr came to town for her uncle's funeral, and hadn't left as she was tying up the last of his affairs. Meanwhile, she claimed she had left the entertainment business and was considering her options for her second act in life.

My father had been all too happy to introduce them.

Sybil didn't remember meeting Collin online, but then again, she was in a lot of internet groups. Apparently, she was a big reader, but never remembered the names of the authors. She was as beautiful as I remembered, with her strawberry-blonde hair and pouty, collagen-enhanced lips, but she had never been as gifted intellectually ... or so I had thought. But hey, to each his own. If she was who Collin wanted, then I would be happy for them both.

Then why did my stomach twist into knots over the thought of them together?

I decided that men were overrated. It would have been nice to have had a 'plus-one' tonight for Tiffany and Matt's wedding, but I would manage like I always did. Alone. The ceremony had been sweet and touching in *Sacred Heart Church,* with all of Matt's family in town from Ireland. Zoe, Harmony, and I, along with Matt's sisters, were Tiffany's bridesmaids, with her twin sister Tabatha as her maid of honor. Chaz and Byron were groomsmen, with Matt's cousin Finn as his best man.

I got paired with Aidan.

Tiffany wore a modern white wedding gown, made of a sleek, satin material that flowed over her curves. The bodice was adorned with delicate lace detailing, and the skirt cascaded down to her feet in soft waves. Matt wore a black tuxedo, with his groomsmen wearing Kelly green, and we bridesmaids were adorned in sleeveless gold silk gowns.

I'd never felt more exposed in my life.

Now that the hour-long ceremony and mass were finished, we gathered in the fully decorated *McGinny's Pub* for the reception.

The walls of the pub were adorned with dark wooden panels, each one carved with intricate Celtic designs. The ceiling was draped with festive streamers in shades of green and gold, reflecting off the warm candlelit tables scattered throughout the room. Lush floral arrangements in shades of white, green, and purple added a touch of elegance to the rustic setting.

The smell of freshly cooked food wafted through the air, mixing with the scent of flowers and the subtle fragrance of candles on the tables. The faint smell of wood and whiskey barrels lingered in the background. The pub was alive with the sound of laughter and lively chatter, with occasional bursts of traditional Irish music adding to the festive atmosphere.

Everything was going splendidly until the pub doors opened.

In walked a dashing Collin Quinn with a stunning Sybil Starr on his arm.

I gasped. "What is he doing here?" I asked Zoe.

"Tiff invited him because she thought you would bring him as your plus-one." She winced. "Sorry. We were all rooting for you two."

"Yeah, what are the odds that Real Sybil would show

up after all these years?" Harmony studied her as they grabbed a couple of drinks and hors d'oeuvres from a passing waiter. "Damn, she looks great."

"I know. I just hope she doesn't figure out that I was innocently impersonating her as Cyber Sybil. In my defense, I really didn't remember her stage name, but that won't matter. Everyone knows I love Oliver King, and Collin mentioned they met in *The King's Quills* chatroom."

"You didn't start reading King until after graduation, and Sybil was never that intuitive. I wouldn't worry. I don't think she'll make the connection." Zoe glanced across the room. "Don't panic, but they're headed our way."

My heart raced as Collin and Sybil approached. I forced a smile, hoping it didn't look as strained as it felt. This dress left nothing to the imagination.

"Morti, it's good to see you," Collin said warmly. His eyes lingered on me for a moment before turning to Zoe and Harmony. "Ladies, you all look lovely tonight."

"Thank you," Zoe replied graciously. "We're so glad you could make it."

Sybil beamed, her perfectly white teeth gleaming. "Isn't this just the most darling wedding? I absolutely adore small town celebrations." She turned to me, her eyes widening slightly. "Oh, my goodness, Morticia Smith? I barely recognized you. It's been ages."

I nodded stiffly. "Good to see you, Sybil. I was sorry to hear about your uncle. Welcome back to Mayflower."

"Thank you, it's so wonderful to be back," Sybil

gushed. "And to think, if it wasn't for poor Uncle Dante's unfortunate accident and leaving me an inheritance, I might never have reconnected with this handsome devil." She squeezed Collin's arm affectionately.

I felt my stomach churn. "Yes, what a ... fortunate turn of events," I managed to say. Reconnect? She'd never even met him before, and wouldn't be his plus-one if it weren't for me. Life was so unfair sometimes.

Collin cleared his throat. "Sybil has been showing me around town, filling me in on all the local gossip. Apparently, her uncle kept her informed in the past, and her childhood friends are only too happy to keep her up-to-date, now that she's back." His gaze locked on mine. "It's been quite enlightening."

"Oh, I'm sure," I muttered under my breath as I looked away, my cheeks heating.

Harmony shot me a concerned look before turning to Sybil with a forced smile. "So, Sybil, what have you been up to since leaving Mayflower? Last we heard you were pursuing a career in ... entertainment?"

Sybil's eyes widened slightly at Harmony's question. She let out a tinkling laugh that sounded rehearsed. "Oh, you know, a little of this, a little of that. I've dabbled in various ... artistic pursuits, but I'm through with all that now." She waved her hand vaguely. "I'm thinking of settling down, maybe opening a little boutique here in Mayflower. What do you think, Collin? Wouldn't that be divine?"

Collin smiled politely. "I'm sure whatever you decide to do will be a success."

I tamped down the green monster growling within me. Of course he would encourage her in whatever she wanted to do. He was that kind of guy. *My* kind of guy.

"Well, we should mingle," Sybil said brightly. "So many people to catch up with. It was lovely seeing you all." She tugged on Collin's arm, leading him away.

As soon as they were out of earshot, I let out a breath I didn't realize I'd been holding.

"Well, that was awkward," Harmony muttered.

"You okay, hon?" Zoe asked gently, placing a hand on my arm.

I nodded, forcing a smile. "I'm fine. Really. It's just ... strange seeing her again after all these years."

"And with Collin," Harmony added bluntly.

I looked at her. "It doesn't matter. We're just friends, and it was a research date ... not a *real* date. He was just being nice with my birthday surprise because he's a nice guy. He doesn't owe me anything. He came here looking for Sybil, and now he's found her. End of story."

Zoe and Harmony exchanged glances that I couldn't quite decipher. Before either of them could say anything more, the DJ announced it was time for the first dance.

We watched as Tiffany and Matt took to the dance floor, swaying to the soft melody of *At Last* by Etta James. They looked blissfully happy, lost in each other's eyes as they moved gracefully across the floor.

As the song ended, the DJ invited other couples to join

them. I watched as Zoe was whisked away by Chaz, and Harmony by Byron. Even my father took to the floor with Samantha. Soon it seemed like everyone was paired off and dancing.

Everyone except me.

I sighed, resigning myself to another wedding spent on the sidelines. At least the bar was open. I made my way over. If ever there was a time to start drinking, tonight would be the night. Who was I kidding? I was terrified of ending up like my mother, and had never touched a drop. I placed my order and sat on a stool.

"I'll have what she's having," a familiar voice said from beside me to the bartender.

I turned to see Collin.

"Two diet colas," the bartender said, setting the glasses in front of us.

Collin raised a dark brow curiously at me before adding, "Can I get a shot of whiskey with that?"

"And a slice of lime with mine, please," I said to the bartender and handed him a tip.

The bartender nodded and quickly prepared our drinks. Collin took a sip of his whiskey and cola, watching me over the rim of his glass.

"Not much of a drinker?" he asked.

I shook my head. "Never touched a drop."

"Now there's an interesting twist. Any particular reason?"

I hesitated, debating how much to share. "My mother died when I was born. Alcohol was involved. End of story."

Collin's expression softened. "I'm sorry. That must have been difficult growing up without her." His face took on a hard edge. "My ex-wife left me for my best friend. Alcohol was involved and still is. Ongoing story."

"I'm sorry, too. It must be difficult moving on for you as well." I shrugged, trying to appear nonchalant. "As for me, it was just my dad and me. We managed just fine without her."

"My ex is still alive, while your mother isn't. It couldn't have been easy then or now." His gray eyes studied me intently. "Is that why you stayed in Mayflower? To be there for your father?"

"Partly," I admitted. "But also because I love this town." I squeezed the lime into my cola, watching the bubbles fizz.

"I think I became a travel writer because the thought of putting down roots reminds me of my ex. I've never had a desire to settle down again until I met Sybil online. She seems so honest and sincere. I love her bluntness. What you see is what you get. I don't think I can handle any more deception."

"Speaking of Sybil, where is she?" I steered the conversation away from deception and swallowed hard, realizing he was going to hate me when he found out I was Cyber Sybil. I didn't stand a chance, so it was best not to even try.

Collin glanced over his shoulder. "Catching up with old classmates, I believe. She certainly knows how to work a room."

I nodded, unsure what to say.

He looked back at me. "It's strange. In person, she seems so different than the woman I met online."

"Oh, how so?" I looked around the room, unable to meet his eyes.

"It's like she's never read Oliver King. She says she has, but I'm beginning to suspect she's just saying that to placate me. Then I remember her messages from the group. Her analysis of King's books was always so insightful." He shrugged. "Who knows. Maybe she used the internet for help with her answers before typing them. All I know is that in person, she seems like a completely different person."

"Maybe she's just nervous around you because you're a King superfan."

His gaze cut to mine. "How do you know that? You've only just joined the group."

I looked away. "Oh, well, I mean I just get that sense from the old threads I read in the group."

An awkward silence fell between us as we sipped our drinks.

"So," Collin finally said, "how are you enjoying the wedding?"

"Oh, it's lovely," I replied automatically. "Tiffany and Matt look so happy."

"They do," he agreed. His gaze swept over the dance floor before landing back on me. "You look beautiful tonight, by the way. That dress suits you."

I felt my ears heat at the compliment. "Thank you," I murmured, suddenly feeling self-conscious in the form-fitting gold bridesmaid dress. I wasn't used to showing so much skin. "You look quite dapper yourself."

Collin smiled, his eyes crinkling at the corners. "Thank you. Though I feel a bit underdressed compared to all the Irish finery on display tonight."

I chuckled, some of the tension easing between us. "True. Matt's family certainly knows how to dress for an occasion."

We fell into a more comfortable silence, people-watching as the reception continued around us. I found my gaze drawn to Collin more often than I cared to admit. There was something about him that intrigued me, despite my best efforts to remain aloof.

"Would you like to dance?" he asked suddenly, setting down his empty glass.

My lips parted in surprise. "Oh, I don't know. I'm not much of a dancer."

"Neither am I," he confessed with a chuckle. "But it seems a shame to let such a lovely dress go to waste standing by the bar all night. What do you say? Shall we stumble around the dance floor together? In the name of research, of course."

"Of course." I laughed. His eyes twinkled with amusement, and I found myself nodding before I could overthink it. "Alright, but don't say I didn't warn you about my two left feet."

Collin offered me his hand.

As I placed my hand in his, I felt a little jolt of electricity.

"There you are," Sybil said.

We dropped our hands simultaneously.

"Come on. They're playing my favorite song." She tugged at his arm.

"Raincheck?" he said over his shoulder as she pulled him away.

I raised my glass in salute and muttered, "Story of my life."

Chapter Six

Harmony stood in the kitchen in her apartment above her new-age shop, *Peace, Love, & Harmony*, with a flour-covered disaster that used to be a batch of chocolate chip cookies on the counter before her. A lone chocolate chip clung to her finger like it was hoping for redemption, while the rest lay scattered about like little brown casualties of war.

It was her turn to host our weekly girls' night, but a baking aficionado she was not.

She sighed dramatically as she wiped her hands on a dishrag. "Maybe we should just skip dessert and order pizza," she suggested, her voice tinged with resignation. "Tiffany's not here to judge us, after all." She winked with a chuckle.

"She does like the finer things in life." Zoe giggled with a grin. "I hope Alaska is treating her well."

"Oh, I'll bet Matt is making sure of that." Harmony

snorted. "She only agreed to Alaska because she knew it was on his bucket list."

"That's true. I took care of Chaz for agreeing to Paris for me." Zoe smirked and then looked at the monstrosity once more. "Maybe we should just eat the cookie rubble?" She plucked a charred piece and held it triumphantly like a trophy, glancing my way with mischief in her eyes. "Morticia's here to judge us instead."

"Hey." I raised my chin a notch, smoothing my black leisure suit. "I don't judge; I merely observe. And I'm observing that Harm is failing spectacularly at this domesticity thing, but kudos for trying."

"Thanks for the vote of confidence," Harm muttered, tossing the burnt remains into the trash with a dramatic sigh.

"You know I'm teasing because of the judgy remarks you girls gave me."

She shrugged. "I know that. My sigh is not over you. I want to bake cookies for Byron before he comes back to town, but clearly, I can't get this recipe right."

"Aww, I told you I would make them for you, hon." Zoe patted Harmony's arm.

"Then they wouldn't be from me." She shrugged as she tossed the cookie sheet into the sink and wiped her hands. "Oh, well. He knew what he was signing up for when he asked me to be his girlfriend."

"Yes, he did." Zoe smiled. "And a great girlfriend you are."

"Speaking of girlfriends," I interjected softly, "Collin's

still with Sybil." My words hung heavy in the air, thickening the atmosphere like fog rolling in over Freedom Lake.

"Ugh, Collin," Harmony scoffed, flicking her fingers dismissively. "You know, babe, you've said you're worried about the whole childbirth thing because of what happened to your mom, but she had health problems. You don't. I think you'd make a great mom, and you don't need a boyfriend for that."

"I don't know." I cringed. "I'm not sure I can just sleep with random guys to get access to their sperm."

"Lucky for you, you don't have to." Zoe nodded. "You don't need a boyfriend. You just need science. Have you thought about the sperm donor idea?"

"Now we're cooking," Harmony quipped. "I can just see Morti in a lab coat, wielding test tubes filled with liquid courage and questionable choices. I love it."

"Well, I am pretty good at going solo with cybersex." I shrugged, warming to the idea. "I can swipe on his profile, pay for his sperm, and impregnate myself. You girls just might be onto something."

"Seriously though." Zoe leaned in. "This could be your chance to take charge of your life. Plus, think of all the amazing stories you will have to tell about being a single mom."

"Or horror stories." I shuddered, rethinking the idea. "Can you imagine? 'Nightmare on Crib Street'?"

"More like 'The Exorcist: Toddler Edition,'" Harmony added, snorting.

"Okay, okay," Zoe interrupted, waving her hands like a conductor trying to orchestrate our chaotic symphony. "What if we brainstorm potential donors? Like a buffet of DNA. We could rate them based on looks, intelligence, and how likely they are to leave you with a lifetime supply of therapy bills."

"That sounds practical. I looked into this a while back, and there are clinics not too far from Mayflower. Some let you search their database online, while others have a book you can take home."

Harmony chuckled. "I can just picture your future child, fueled by a cocktail of genetic quirks and literary references, asking, 'Mommy, who's my daddy?'"

"And I'll answer, 'Well, darling, he's a tall, dark stranger, with a quick wit and great genes.'" I blinked. "Good Lord, I could be describing Collin Quinn.'"

"Now there's a thought. Collin Quinn as your baby daddy." Zoe winked.

"Or not." I shook my head, even as a shiver zipped up my spine. A sperm bank was sounding better by the second.

"Let's do it. Let's draw up a list of qualities," Harmony declared, her enthusiasm infectious. "We can even create a dating app profile for Morticia—'Swipe right for mother-hood.' I'll host."

"Only if it comes with a guarantee of edible snacks," Zoe deadpanned, her eyes twinkling. "What do you say, Morti? Are you in?"

"Okay," I blurted, before I could change my mind,

laughter bubbling up inside me, the tension easing like clouds fading away to sunlight. In that moment, surrounded by my friends, my crazy life felt oddly manage-able—and maybe, just maybe, so did the prospect of diving headfirst into the unknown waters of parenthood without a life raft ... or a partner.

AFTER DOING extensive research and carefully picking a sperm donor facility, I signed up. I'd already had my first appointment, and picked up their binder full of potential donors to bring home and make my decision. I'd called the girls for an emergency meeting and arranged for them to drop everything and come over to help me. They did with no questions asked.

It's how we rolled.

Now that they were here, I reached into my bag and pulled out the binder, its weight suddenly feeling like a ton of bricks in my hands. "So, uh, this is it," I said, my voice barely above a whisper. "The catalog of potential baby daddies."

Zoe's eyes widened. "Oh, my goodness, it's like a menu for making humans."

"More like a genetic buffet," Harmony countered, leaning in closer.

I flipped open the binder, revealing page after page of smiling faces and carefully curated profiles. "I've narrowed it down to these top contenders, but I'm ... I'm kind of overwhelmed."

Tiffany, still glowing from her Alaskan honeymoon, peered over my shoulder. "Ooh, look at Mr. Tall, Dark, and Doctorate in Neuroscience. Imagine the brain on that baby."

As we huddled over the binder, giggling and debating the merits of various donors, I couldn't shake the feeling that we were playing some bizarre game of "Frankenstein." It was exhilarating and terrifying all at once.

"What about this one?" Zoe pointed to a profile. "He's got your love for literature and—"

"Ladies, what's all the secrecy about?"

I nearly jumped out of my skin at the sound of Collin's voice behind us. In our donor-induced frenzy, we hadn't noticed his approach. I slammed the binder shut, my heart pounding like a trapped bat in my chest.

"Collin!" I squeaked, trying to sound nonchalant and failing miserably. "We were just, um ..."

"Planning world domination," Harmony interjected smoothly. "You know, the usual Tuesday afternoon activity."

Collin's eyes darted from face to face, his expression a mix of amusement and curiosity. "And that requires a secret meeting behind the funeral home?"

I took a deep breath, steeling myself. "Actually, Collin, I'm looking into having a baby. On my own."

His eyebrows shot up and some unreadable expression flashed. "Oh. Wow. That's ... unexpected."

"Is it?" I found myself saying, a sudden surge of frustration giving me courage. "I'm tired of waiting for the perfect moment, the perfect man. Just when I think one is available, it turns out he's not. Life's too short, you know?"

Collin frowned then nodded slowly, his gaze softening. "I get it. Life has a way of slipping by if we're not careful."

An awkward silence fell over us, heavy with unspoken words and missed opportunities.

Finally, unable to bear it any longer, I blurted, "So, um, how's Sybil doing?"

Collin's expression shifted, the flicker of warmth in his stormy gray eyes dimming slightly as the name hung in the air like a thundercloud. "She's, um, doing well. Decided she wants to try writing a novel instead of opening a boutique, as if they're even remotely comparable. I think she's trying to impress me." His voice faltered slightly. "She's really dedicated to learning the craft. I'll give her that." He shrugged, but there was a tightness in his shoulders that suggested Sybil's endeavors weighed heavier on him than he let on.

"Good for her," I replied, attempting to inject some enthusiasm into my voice. "I mean, it must be nice to have that kind of creative outlet." Pretending I cared about her latest escapades felt absurd.

"Yeah," he replied flatly, clearly still caught between two worlds—the allure of the mysterious Sybil and the daunting reality of my unfiltered honesty. "It's just different talking to someone who exists only behind a screen than it is in person."

I understood that all too well. "Ah, the glorious world of fiction writers," I said, my tone laced with irony. "It must be nice to escape into a world where the protagonists don't have to worry about mundane things like ... you know, having babies. But I guess we all can't be like Oliver King."

"Yeah," he replied quietly, his eyes drifting towards the ground as if contemplating the weight of my words. "Fiction can be easier than reality sometimes."

Zoe cleared her throat. "So, Morti was just telling us about her potential baby daddies."

Harmony leaned in closer to Collin, a conspiratorial glint in her eye as she tapped the binder. "Wanna join our little genetic buffet?"

I gasped, feeling my cheeks flood with heat as I shot both Harmony and Zoe a mortified look.

Collin looked from Zoe to Harmony to me, amusement creeping back into his eyes as he shoved his hands into the pockets of his tailored slacks, an air of nonchalance settling over him. "Not sure you want these old genes." He laughed, but there was curiosity shimmering in his eyes. "Tell me about this whole baby thing? Have you—"

"I've done a bit of research," I interjected, desperate to steer the conversation away from anything too personal. "Just flipping through profiles and seeing who might potentially qualify for the—uh, job. It's like auditioning for a part in a play where the script hasn't been written yet." I glanced back at the binder, feeling almost vulnerable, as if I were laying bare my innermost desires to everyone present.

"You know, traits that would make for a well-rounded human being."

"What kind of 'traits' are we talking about?" Collin asked, his eyebrows arched in amusement. "A fondness for coffins and coffee shop poetry?"

"Oh, definitely," Harmony piped up, nodding enthusiastically. "And books, of course."

Laughter bubbled up again, but I felt a twinge of discomfort at how freely they teased the very real decisions I was contemplating. "I mean, I'm looking for someone who is at least moderately functional," I said half-heartedly, glancing at Collin who wore an intrigued look.

He raised an eyebrow. "Maybe someone with good cooking skills? An affinity for literary debates?"

"Oh, that would be a bonus," I replied, warming to the absurdity of the situation. "But mostly someone with good genes—literally. You know, the usual stuff."

"Right," he said, leaning in just a bit closer, his expressive eyes narrowing. "How about a sense of humor? Maybe someone outgoing."

Harmony grinned, elbowing me lightly. "Oh, that's vital. We don't want your future child to be yet another *Smith Funeral Home* introvert."

Collin studied me curiously.

The air crackled with a blend of levity and something deeper. My palms began to sweat under his gaze, a strange warmth unfurling in the pit of my stomach as if he had ignited a spark I'd long thought extinguished.

"I agree, another introvert probably wouldn't be the

best idea," I replied, trying to keep my tone casual even as my heart raced with potential.

"Oh, I don't know." Collin's gaze locked onto mine. "I find the most fascinating people to be introverts."

Zoe leaned back, looking between the two of us. "And what exactly are you saying, Collin?"

"Just that outgoing can be overrated. No mystery," he countered smoothly, never breaking eye contact. "Sometimes introverts can be surprising. Have depth that reveals itself only when provoked."

I stifled a laugh. I often hid behind walls of books and sarcasm. "Poking an introvert might not be wise. The outcome's so unpredictable." I folded my arms defensively across the binder while trying to project an image of nonchalance.

"But worth it, I imagine."

His words hung in the air. I could feel the weight of his observation settle over me, like a warm quilt knitted from threads of understanding and camaraderie.

"Right." I scoffed. "Because there's nothing more alluring than a woman who talks to dead bodies for a living."

"Hey," Zoe chimed in, her voice laced with mock indignation. "We all have our quirks. Some people collect stamps; you collect stories from the dearly departed."

"I don't collect stories from *them*." I shrugged. "I just like to learn about who they were, so I research them. You know, for the obituary."

"Careful, there. They just might stick around to haunt you," Collin stated, with a sparkle in his eye.

We all fell into laughter again. But inside, my heart fluttered at the way he seemed to genuinely appreciate my peculiarities rather than judge them.

"You're one interesting woman, Morticia." Collin studied me.

"Is that a compliment?" I asked, raising an eyebrow in mock suspicion.

"I'm just saying introverts have layers, like an onion or a really good lasagna."

"Lasagna?" Zoe's eyes twinkled with mischief. "Morti, if you're going to create a life, you might as well ensure he or she has the potential for a well-rounded palate."

"Well, I'm not sure about taste buds yet," I countered, "but I'm considering character traits over culinary skills."

Collin chuckled softly. "Hey, if they take after their mother, they're bound to turn out just fine. Little research geniuses."

My cheeks flushed at the term 'mother.' It felt foreign and exhilarating simultaneously. "I sure hope so."

As our banter subsided, an uncomfortable thought flickered through my mind, Would Collin ever see me as more than just a research assistant? As if the universe were answering, Collin's phone rang.

He glanced at the caller ID, and his smile slipped. "It's Sybil. Good luck, ladies." He lifted the phone to his ear as he walked away.

And just like that, the clouds returned to the sky, blocking out the sun.

Chapter Seven

The moment I stepped into the coffee shop one week later, the scent of burnt beans assaulted my senses. I scanned the room, looking for that rare artifact known as a comfortable seat—preferably one that wasn't occupied by someone who smelled like they had bathed in an ill-conceived cologne, or worse yet, reminiscent of last week's fish special at *Lolita's Place*.

Truman was having coffee with Gerty and Gabby, smiling wide as he recanted stories, and they laughed at all his jokes. I smiled on the inside. Maybe me being busy wasn't such a bad thing after all.

Collin sat in the corner with Harmony, his intense gray eyes peering over a stack of papers that looked far too orderly for this town. He was scribbling notes as if he were drafting the next great American novel rather than an article about Mayflower's haunted past. My heart stuttered —an irregular beat of both dread and fascination—as I contemplated whether to approach him or retreat behind the safety of my reclusive persona.

"Morti!" Harmony's voice cut through the fog of my indecision. She waved me over with an enthusiasm that might earn her a spot on a morning talk show—or late night, considering it was Harm we were talking about. "Dude, you've got to join us. Collin was just sharing some wild tales about the ghost at the old lighthouse. He did some research after you told him about it."

"Cool." I took a deep breath, reminding myself that avoiding social situations would not help me in my quest for motherhood—or for whatever else I was secretly craving. I made my way over, striving to appear nonchalant while assessing every potential hazard along the path: spilled coffee, an overzealous toddler, or worse, the lurking presence of Mr. Fish Special himself.

I hesitated halfway to them, weighing the idea of sliding into the booth and breaking down my carefully constructed defenses against potential heart palpitations. But the thought of letting Harm down propelled me forward, each step like a mini triumph over my anxiety.

"Uh, hey," I mumbled, sliding into the worn leather seat across from Collin. I fought to keep my expression casual, though I could feel his eyes lingering longer than necessary.

"Hey there yourself," Collin greeted me with a genuine smile that set my insides buzzing. "You're just in time. Harmony was telling me about her fortune-teller tools to summon the spirits. I want to try it out, and you did agree to help me with more research. So, when do you want to take that tour?"

I glanced at my watch. "We'll have to schedule that. I have a date with some sperm." My face flushed red as I realized I'd said that last part out loud.

He arched a black brow high, his smile slipping slightly. "So, you chose a donor I'm guessing."

Harm slapped her palm on the table, jostling their coffees. "Yay. I'm so excited for you. Who did you end up going with?"

I swallowed, suddenly feeling like I was on trial. "I chose the philosopher. There were a bunch of steps I had to do to make sure I am one-hundred-percent ready. It's a whole process," I stammered, wishing I could sink into the cushions. "It's all a bit daunting."

Collin leaned forward, his expression shifting to one of genuine curiosity. "What's daunting about it? Isn't it just like picking out a book? You read the cover, check the blurb, maybe even flip through a few pages?"

"Except this book comes with DNA and a lifetime commitment," I countered, the gravity of my words pulling me deeper into my own churning thoughts.

Harmony chimed in, waving her hands theatrically. "It's like choosing a partner without the whole messy emotional baggage. Think of it as shopping for an accessory—just way more complicated."

"That's why I have to get going. The sperm bank has the frozen sperm I chose ready, and today's the perfect day."

Collin frowned, glancing out the window at the rainy weather. "What makes today perfect?"

My face again flushed crimson as I thought, no rubbers or raincoat needed on this date. I opened and closed my mouth, unable to form coherent words.

He looked at me and his eyes widened. "Ahh, it's all in the timing I hear."

"You would be right." I stood. "So, raincheck on the haunted lighthouse tour." I turned and left as quickly as possible before my face burned off, hearing Harm's remark, 'Good luck to your little swimmers.'

Rushing to Fester, it took me the entire hour drive to Boston to calm my racing heart.

Gripping the binder in my hands, I dashed inside the clinic and signed in. I had already met with the donor coordination team and gone over the instructions for handling and storing the sperm sample. Today, client services brought me into a room and went over how to thaw the sperm and how to use the home insemination kit.

"Any questions?" a staff member asked me?

Yeah, what the hell am I doing? I wanted to say, but I swallowed my comment and shook my head.

"It's okay, honey." She squeezed my cold hand. "Everyone gets nervous the first time, but it's really not that bad. Just be prepared that it might not work this way. If it doesn't and you want to try again, you can always go through insemination at a facility or even your own OB-GYN office."

"Thank you." I took my sample and headed home,

thinking diet cola wasn't gonna cut it to set the mood and prepare me for what I was about to do.

SEVERAL DAYS HAD PASSED since that awkward self-insemination day. The process was more involved than I had imagined.

"Samantha, I didn't expect to see you here." I stopped short in the parking lot of our funeral home, waiting for Collin.

As promised, I was taking him on a tour of the haunted lighthouse today. Dad had agreed to cover for me at work, in exchange for me finally planning his bachelor party. I had been putting him off for a while now, hoping he would change his mind about marrying Samantha. The wedding was in five months, and they didn't look like they were slowing down on the planning process one bit.

She stepped out of my father's new sports car and joined him by the curb. "Why wouldn't I come? We do everything together, don't we, Pooh Bear?"

"That we do, my love." He kissed her cheek, then dabbed his sweaty brow with a handkerchief.

Collin stepped outside at that moment. "Evening, Mr. Smith." He shook my father's hand and then bowed his head to Samantha. "Nice to see you again, Ms. Somerville."

Great. Even Collin knew her last name. I really was a horrible daughter.

"Take care of my girl," my father said to Collin. "She's never sick, but she didn't come into work at all the other day."

Oh, good lord.

That was when I was doing my self-insemination and had to stay in bed a while. My father didn't like to talk about me having a baby, especially on my own, since my mother had died during childbirth. I admitted it made me a little nervous as well, but I kept reminding myself that I wasn't my mother. I hadn't told him I had decided to go with a sperm doner because I didn't want to worry him, so I'd called in sick instead of telling him what I was really up to.

He hadn't stopped worrying since.

"Well, nothing like a date with some good ole-fashioned bed rest to cure what ails one." Collin's lips twitched as he shot a knowing look in my direction.

I could feel my ears burn off. "Yes, well, I'm feeling much better, Dad."

He eyed my red face warily. "Are you sure?"

"Positive." I grabbed Collin's hand and tugged him toward Fester. "Gotta run. We have a date with a haunted lighthouse."

We reached my hearse, and I realized I was still holding Collin's hand.

His smile widened. "Layers," he said, for my ears only.

I rolled my eyes and dropped his hand.

"We'd better hit the road if we're going to get there

before dark. Everything creepy seems to take place on the outskirts of town." I slid into the driver's seat.

"Don't we want it to be dark, so the ghost makes an appearance?" He climbed into the passenger side.

"Yes, but I'd like to get there while it's still light out." I hated driving in the dark.

We drove in awkward silence for a while, but then I couldn't take it anymore. "So, how's Sybil?"

A brief, amused silence filled the car.

Collin's fingers drummed lightly against the dash as he glanced sideways at me, and I could almost see the gears turning in his head. "Sybil is ... well, she's been keeping me entertained," he said, drawing out his words as if they were pieces of a puzzle he was still trying to fit together. "But you know, she doesn't quite compare to the Sybil I met in our group online. That's why I keep sticking around, hoping to see a glimpse of her again. *That* Sybil was clever, quick witted ... she challenged me." He glanced at me pensively. "Kind of like you."

I kept my hands locked on the steering wheel. My heart did a little jig before my brain caught up and told it to simmer down. "I can't believe you're actually saying that," I replied, feigning disbelief while my pulse quickened. "Online, we're all free to be whoever we choose to be. A fictional character, so to speak. Maybe she's afraid you'll see beyond the facade in real life. Do you often compare fictional characters to real-life people? That seems like a slippery slope."

His stormy eyes sparkled with mischief. "Oh, very slippery, but then again, not everyone in the group is fictional. Take you, for instance. What you see is what you get. Your avatar is a coffin and in real life you actually drive around in a hearse."

"All I'm saying is, not everyone is comfortable in their own skin."

"Believe me, that's not Sybil's problem. She's turning into a bit of a diva lately. I think she's convinced she's going to become a best seller with her first book, and have her own book-signing tour or something."

"Of course she is," I muttered, feeling a strange swell of jealousy claw at my insides. I wasn't sure if it was over the thought of her finishing an actual book, or dating Collin Quinn, my two biggest fantasies.

Collin chuckled, his eyes flickering with a mix of amusement and something deeper, something that made my heart race. "She just wrote this crazy plot twist where the main character falls for the ghost haunting her house. She's surprisingly not bad."

"Sounds like a real page-turner," I replied, trying to keep my tone light even as the green monster gnawed at my insides. What was it about Sybil that intrigued him so? Was it the allure of mystery? Or was it simply that she was everything I wasn't—confident, carefree, and completely unbothered?

"Speaking of interesting stories," he said, turning to me with a teasing glint in his eye, "what's your deal with using a sperm donor? I mean, I get the appeal—new life and all— but it's pretty unconventional."

I swallowed hard as the truth of my situation loomed over me like the haunting specter of the lighthouse we were driving toward. "It's not about being unconventional, Collin," I said, my voice barely above a whisper. "It's about taking control of my life, you know? I'm tired of waiting around for things to happen. It's time I make something happen." My heart thudded against my ribcage as I spoke.

Collin furrowed his brow, his fingers drumming an anxious rhythm against the dashboard. "I know I asked what's so daunting about choosing a donor, but don't you worry about having a baby alone? You're kind of ... diving head-first into uncharted waters. What if it doesn't work out?" He shot me a sideways glance, his eyes shadowed with concern.

"And what if it does?" I countered, surprised by the assertiveness in my own voice. "What if it leads to something beautiful?" I couldn't believe I was defending my decision with such passion.

"But what's driving you to do this alone? You're a beautiful, intelligent, fascinating woman. You could have any man you wanted if you let down your walls and put yourself out there."

Not anyone. Not you.

I was silent for a beat too long, caught in the crosshairs of his gaze, an intense scrutiny that felt like being examined under a magnifying glass. I cleared my throat. "Oh, look. There's the lighthouse." I parked Fester in the parking lot and cut the engine just as the sun was setting over the coast. The place looked deserted when it was supposed to be open for tours.

That was odd.

The lighthouse loomed ahead, its silhouette stark against the twilight sky, a darkened sentinel watching over the waves crashing defiantly at its base. "Haunted" was an understatement; it looked like a place where secrets were buried deep and whispered into the wind.

The fading light spilled golden rays across the rocky shore, casting long shadows that seemed to dance along with the crashing waves. As I stepped out of the hearse, the salty breeze tousled strands that had escaped my tightly pinned hair, and I felt an unexpected flutter of excitement mingled with anxiety.

"Sorry that it's not open, but I can at least show you around outside." I led the way.

Collin followed, his hands stuffed in his pockets, and for a moment, it was just us—two lone figures against the twilight. "That's okay. I'm more interested in the story behind this place. I've read the research, but some of it is vague. What's your take on what really happened here?" he asked, tilting his head as he surveyed the lighthouse.

"Legend has it that a lighthouse keeper fell in love with a mermaid who lived in the ocean below," I began, channeling my inner tour guide as we walked the grounds. "They would meet beneath the light of the moon, until one fateful night when a storm rolled in. She was swept away and never returned."

"Romantic but tragic," he said, staring at the towering

structure that stood ominously against the darkening sky. "It looks like something straight out of a horror novel."

"Or a really bad tourist brochure," I replied, attempting to mask the way my heart was thrumming at his proximity. "But trust me, the real horror is what's lurking inside."

He chuckled softly, tilting his head as he studied me with those eyes that could hold both mischief and sincerity. "Is it ghosts, or just *your* ghosts haunting you?"

"Ah, a bit of both, I suppose," I said, crossing my arms defensively against the chill in the air. For a travel writer, he seemed to ask a lot of personal questions. The lighthouse looked like a beacon for all those unresolved issues that kept me from embracing the life I thought I wanted. "They say the keeper's spirit still roams these shores, searching for his lost love. I can relate to that," I continued.

Collin took a step closer, his gaze piercing through the evening fog wrapping around us like a shroud. "What are you searching for? A lost love ... or your mother's lingering ghost?"

The audacity of his question sent a shiver down my spine—not from fear, but from the sudden pull of raw vulnerability. I wasn't ready to dissect my tangled emotions about motherhood or my family; they were more like lead weights than feathers.

"Maybe just a little clarity," I replied, deflecting with a wry smile that didn't quite reach my eyes. I stared at the lighthouse, its peeling paint and rusted lantern a metaphor for all my frayed edges. "The ghosts of my past are like unwelcome visitors; they never really leave. Just linger around the corners of my mind, waiting for the right moment to creep back in."

Collin's expression softened, and for a heartbeat, it felt as if he could see right through the layers I'd painstakingly built around myself. "I get that," he said quietly, stepping closer to me as if caught in some magnetic pull. "But you don't have to face them alone."

Alone.

The word echoed in my brain like a drumbeat, reminding me of everything I'd fought against. I turned to him, my heart doing that ridiculous dance again. "Not all of us are lucky enough to have found someone."

"Ah, but finding the *right* someone ... well, that remains to be seen." He studied me, then suddenly looked away.

I opened my mouth to comment, but something in Collin's expression stopped me. "What's wrong?"

His gaze surveyed the area like Sherlock Holmes. "Ever since I got to town, I've had this niggling sensation that someone is watching me. *Following* me."

I laughed. "Well, you *have* been ghost hunting. That certainly breeds an active imagination. Maybe our light-house keeper is here after all."

"Maybe," he mused, sounding uncertain as he continued to search the area, "but I'm not convinced. In my experience, my hunches are usually right."

Chills ran up my spine as I found myself looking around as well. "Then maybe it's time to go."

"Agreed." He frowned. "I'd say we've had enough visits

from ghosts of the past and present. If it's all the same to you, I don't care to meet any ghosts of the future."

"I never did like spoilers." I pulled out my keys and we headed to Fester, not feeling comfortable until we were safely locked inside the hearse. I almost laughed at the absurdity of that thought, as I started the vehicle and headed back to the funeral home.

Chapter Eight

Another week went by.

I'd hardly seen Collin, and when I did, Sybil was with him. It was almost as if she was jealous of me for helping him with his research. I let my hair down, and it fell to my waist as I ran my fingers over my scalp then the back of my neck, trying to ease the tension. Work was busy, Dad was nonexistent, and I was tired. Slipping on soft, dark-gray yoga pants and a light-gray t-shirt, I left my feet bare and curled up on my couch. Opening my laptop, I logged into my happy place.

The King's Quills

Stacy Rose: *I can't believe Sybil Starr is in Mayflower with you. How is she?*

Collin Quinn: *Different than I expected.*

Stacy Rose: *I miss her. We had a real bond. Did she say if she's coming back to our group?*

Collin Quinn: *Not right now. She's in mourning.*

She Wolf: *Sorry about that for her, but again, not fair. Now Collin has seen both Morti and Sybil.*

Marky Mouse: *Is she there with you now? Either of them?*

Collin Quinn: *No. I'm not sure where Morti is. Ah, there she is. I see you online, Morti, but you've yet to chime in. As for Sybil, she's at her uncle's place, working on her novel. She's his only living relative and still hasn't decided what to do with his house.*

I sucked in a sharp breath, knowing he was right next door ... alone. My fingers hovered over my keyboard, but I didn't know what to say.

Tie Die Dotty: *The poor dear. She's going to need a little TLC when the dust settles.*

Captain Rogers: *Or a little vacation on The Wind-jammer. I'll sail the landlubber away into the sunset while you wipe her tears. What do you say, Dotty? Care to be my first mate?*

Tie Die Dotty: *I prefer grass, but I don't mind a little water now and again.*

Morticia Smith: *I say that's a great idea. Take her mind off her troubles.*

I quickly interjected, seizing the chance to get the real Sybil out of town.

Collin Quinn: *Well, well, Morti's alive after all.*

Morticia Smith: *Barely.*

Collin Quinn: *Sounds like you need a little R and R yourself.*

Tie Die Dotty: *You two will make the perfect crew!*

Captain Rogers: *Aye, matey! All we need is some rum and a little sea shanty to raise our spirits!*

I bit my lip, staring at the screen, a cascade of emotions flooding through me. The thought of being on a boat with Collin—feeling the wind in my hair and the sun warming my skin—was intoxicating. But what would Sybil think of me tagging along? What would she feel? Were they even an official couple? The point was to get her out of town, not have Collin and me join her.

If I were being honest, this felt more like an escape from my own reality than sympathy for a grieving wannabe writer.

The chat buzzed around me, laughter echoing from digital avatars I knew well but had never met or even seen, other than Collin. I imagined them all sailing along with us, sharing stories under the stars. I made a joke about it. Of course, Collin one-upped me with a joke of his own, which led to us sparring back and forth. For a moment, it felt like old times when I was Cyber Sybil.

She Wolf: *You're funny, Morti. I like you.*

Morticia Smith: *Someone has to keep the group entertained, right?*

Stacy Rose: *Exactly! You've been quiet lately. I like this side of you.*

Hans Brewmeister: *Quiet is better than all you chatterboxes. Can we get back to talking about Oliver King? This group isn't The Love Boat.*

Captain Rogers: *But wouldn't it be more fun if it*

were? I swear I could hear the romantic tension crackling between Morti and Collin from here!

Tie Die Dotty: *Sounds like Hans needs a little something to make him relax, and I've got just the thing.*

My heart raced at the unexpected attention, and I could feel my cheeks heating up as I typed furiously, desperately trying to steer the conversation back to safety.

Morticia Smith: *You're all ridiculous. The only tension here is the one in my yoga pants from sitting too long.*

Collin Quinn: *Morticia Smith in yoga pants? Now there's a sight I can't imagine seeing.*

I could imagine him leaning back in his chair, a teasing smirk dancing on his lips. Each notification sent my pulse racing like a priest late for a funeral.

Morticia Smith: *You're just saying that because you've only seen me dressed for the "job." I can be casual when the occasion calls for it.*

Thank God I could hide behind my avatar.

Collin Quinn: *Maybe. Or maybe casual is overrated. I'm starting to think your "job" makes you even more intriguing.*

With that, I logged off.

My hands shook and I inhaled several deep breaths to relax. I headed to my kitchen to make hot white chocolate, even though it was late August and still warm outside. I kept my air conditioner almost as cold as the morgue in our funeral home, because I was always overheated, so hot drinks were never an issue.

A soft knock sounded on my door.

I blinked and my hand jerked, sloshing my white chocolate drink over the side. Yelping, I shook my burned hand and ran it under cold water.

The door opened, and in rushed a concerned Collin.

I gasped, feeling exposed even though I was fully dressed. Still, my hair was down. I never let my hair down for anyone. "Do you always walk inside someone else's apartment before being invited?"

"I heard your cry of pain. Are you okay?" He inspected my hand, then grabbed some ice from my freezer as if he were in his own place. Wrapping the ice in a towel, he held it against the burn spot on my hand.

"Sorry. I just wasn't expecting anyone. I'm not exactly put together. So, um, what brings you here? Aside from my tragic culinary mishap?"

"It sounded like a dare, telling me I hadn't seen you in anything other than your work attire. What can I say? I never could resist a dare." His gaze ran over me from head to toe, then lingered on my hair. "I changed my mind. Casual suits you. You look great. Ethereal, even. What's the occasion? A secret meeting with your donor?"

I flinched at that, though he meant it lightheartedly. The topic always hung like an awkward cloud in the room, and I wasn't ready to dive into that abyss with him—especially not now, not while he was so close. "You know me. Just trying to channel my inner goddess ... or maybe just a literary character too consumed with angst."

He chuckled softly, and for a split second, the tension

in my shoulders eased. "Well, if you're channeling anyone, Morti, let it be someone who knows how to enjoy life. How about we do something? A spontaneous adventure before Sybil shows up and takes over all my time?"

The thought sent my heart racing again—an actual adventure with Collin, not just a research assignment? The heat spread from my cheeks to my entire body, and I suddenly felt trapped in that moment, caught between the weight of my awkwardness and the alluring possibility that maybe—just maybe—there was something more here than mere friendship.

My breath hitched somewhere between my throat and my stomach as I contemplated the implications of accepting his offer. "What did you have in mind?"

"Collin, there you are!" Sybil charged into my apartment, her gaze snapping between his and mine. "I've been calling you over and over, but you didn't answer."

He frowned, looking annoyed, if I didn't know better. "I don't answer my phone when I'm working, and then I left it in my apartment."

"And why aren't *you* in your apartment?" She crossed her arms and pouted.

I held up my burned hand. "Culinary crisis."

"Collin is such a hero, isn't he?" Her smile didn't reach her eyes.

"He sure is." I nodded.

"Well, if you're done, Collin, I have a literary crisis and a novel in need of saving. Can you be *my* hero?"

His face looked calm and patient, as if he were

speaking to a child. "Well, how can I say no to that?" He glanced at me with an unreadable expression. "Bye, Morti. Take care of that hand."

"I will and thank you." I waved with my good hand as he closed the door, shutting off any possibility of us being more than friends.

I frowned, not sure how I felt about that.

A WEEK LATER, I sat in Dr. Joy's office, holding back tears as she delivered the news I had been dreading. "So, what you're saying is I'm not pregnant?"

The doctor nodded sympathetically. "No, I'm sorry."

I closed my eyes and took a deep breath, trying to hold back the flood of emotions threatening to overwhelm me. This wasn't how it was supposed to be. I had been so sure that my late period was a sign that my dream of becoming a mother was finally coming true.

But now, reality crashed down on me once again, shattering my hopes into a million pieces.

"Our bodies can sometimes fool us into thinking we are, if we want it so badly," Dr. Joy continued gently, placing a hand on my shoulder in comfort. "I'm not saying you can't get pregnant, but given your age and a few other factors, I think you might need some help."

"What does that mean?" I asked quietly, already knowing the answer but needing to hear it from her.

"Fertility treatments," she replied simply.

My heart sank even further. I had always known that getting pregnant at forty would be difficult, but I never imagined it would come to this.

"Like what?" I asked, feeling defeated and exhausted.

"Medicine and shots to help your eggs be viable for the next time you try another sperm donor," Dr. Joy explained kindly. "And this time, why don't you come here? Your chances of conceiving go up with professional help."

I knew she was right. Collin had mentioned the same thing before—that seeking professional help instead of going it alone could increase my chances of getting pregnant—but the thought of going through invasive procedures and expensive treatments only added to my anxiety. He was trying to be a helpful, supportive friend, but he always acted strange whenever I brought up the topic of me trying to get pregnant by using a sperm donor.

I couldn't let myself entertain why.

I shook off that thought and focused back on Dr. Joy. Taking a page from Collin's book, I replied, "Well, how can I say no to that?" I forced a small smile, trying to appear optimistic. But deep down, a part of me was spiraling into a dark place, one where ambition and fear twisted together like vines choking the tree of life. "I'll think about it," I amended, my voice sounding more like a whisper in the room that felt too small for the weight of my disappointment.

Dr. Joy gave me a reassuring nod, her demeanor gentling further. "Remember, Morti, hope is not lost. It's just ... delayed."

Delayed.

It felt cruelly appropriate, as if everything in my life had been on a *pause* button, while everyone around me hit *play.* I blinked back tears, my heart heavy with unfulfilled dreams and decisions yet to come.

"Morti, it's okay to feel sad about this," Dr. Joy encouraged, her eyes softening with understanding. "It's a tough journey, but you're not alone in it. We'll keep reassessing and figure this out together."

A bitter knot formed in my stomach. "I know," I whispered, feeling raw and exposed as I tried to process the reality of my situation. "It's just ... I keep picturing this little life that might never be. It feels like I'm chasing shadows."

"Chasing shadows is how a lot of us start out," she replied philosophically, gathering her paperwork as I contemplated the meaning of her words. "But remember, the shadows teach us about light." She nodded once. "Don't lose hope. Not yet."

I nodded back, trying to hang onto the hope she offered as I exited her office, while fear gripped my heart like a vice. I walked through the familiar streets of Mayflower, my mind a storm of thoughts circling Collin and Sybil.

Where was *my* happy ending?

The sun cast its late afternoon glow over the town square, but I felt more like those shadows I'd been chasing moving through it, a ghost haunting the places that used to bring me joy. When I reached home, the silence welcomed me back like an old friend, yet it felt cruel and suffocating in its familiarity. My yoga mat lay sprawled on the floor where I had left it last week—an abandoned lifeboat in a sea of uncertainty.

I sank onto the mat and buried my face in my hands.

Chapter Nine

It was early September, and the Harvest Festival was in full swing. I could empathize with my father. My hormones were all over the place: one minute laughing, the next minute furious, then suddenly sobbing.

Fertility treatments were no joke.

The festival was held in the park, with food trucks, craft tents, and games like bobbing for apples. Finn was playing his guitar and singing Irish tunes on the stage by the gazebo, with Tiffany's sister, Tabatha, watching. Chaz and Zoe, Harmony and Byron, and Matt and Tiffany were saving a spot for me at a table so I wouldn't have to sit with my father and Mommy Dearest, or worse ... Collin and Sybil.

I couldn't deal with their happiness right now.

Zoe's parents and in-laws were up from Florida and Alabama, sitting with Chaz's parents, Tiffany's parents, and Harmony's parents at a table. I passed Truman with

Gerty and Gabby Rogers, laughing and looking happier than ever. They sat at another table with Mayor Edwards, his wife Eleanor, Judge Zander Jackson, lawyers Victoria Steele and Alexandra Knight, Principal Brimstone, and his wife Bitsy.

As I approached my friends' table, their laughter bubbled up like a cheerful effervescence, in stark contrast to my stormy thoughts. The radiant festival lights twinkled overhead, casting a warm, inviting glow that felt entirely at odds with the gnawing emptiness inside me. I took a deep breath, trying to muster a smile for them—my lifelines.

I seriously didn't know what I would do without them.

"Morti!" Zoe called out, her caramel curls bouncing as she waved me over enthusiastically with a huge smile on her heart-shaped face. "We saved you some pumpkin spice donuts. You're going to love them, hon."

"Yum," I murmured, plopping onto the bench beside a glowing Tiffany. Motherhood suited her.

"Hi, doll." She immediately leaned in conspiratorially, her periwinkle blue eyes sparkling. "You look like you've seen the grim reaper."

"You've just described most of my past dates," I replied dryly, grabbing a donut and forcing it to my mouth as if it could fill the gaping hole in my heart. And honestly, it worked for about thirty seconds.

"Hey, babe!" Harmony chimed in, her spiky red hair glowing like autumn leaves in the sun, and her green cat-eyes narrowing devilishly. "We saved you a cupcake, too. It has more sprinkles than frosting—just how you like it."

I glanced at the colorful confections lined up on the table like confetti, and felt a pang of affection mixed with sadness hit me hard. "Thanks guys, but you know sprinkles won't solve my problems, right?"

"Maybe not," Chaz said with a chuckle, his arm draped casually over Zoe's shoulders. "But they might distract you from it for a minute or two." His smile dimmed as he donned his doctor face. "You look a little flushed?"

"Flushed? I'm just in the throes of a donut-induced sugar rush," I retorted, gesturing with my half-eaten pastry. "Well, that and this whole fertility fiasco. Gotta love hormones."

The laughter around me faded momentarily, the air shifting as my friends exchanged concerned glances. Byron and Matt's grins faltered, and I could feel the weight of their collective empathy pressing down like an unwelcome hug.

Great. *Pity.* Just what I needed.

"Okay, Morti," Zoe said carefully, her voice turning serious. "You can talk to us. You know that, right? We're here for you."

"I know." I sighed, the battle in my heart raging on. I swallowed hard, the sweetness of the donut thickening in my throat. "I appreciate that. It's just …"

My voice trailed off as I caught sight of Collin standing near the stage, laughing with Sybil. She was draped against him like a vine clinging to a trellis, her radiant smile so blindingly perfect that it made my stomach twist like a tornado of regret.

I took another bite of the donut, chewing slowly as I felt my friends' eyes scrutinize me, each of them keenly aware that beneath my veneer of forced humor lay an ocean of uncertainty. "I'm fine, really. Just ... overwhelmed."

"*Overwhelmed* is a good word for it," Tiffany chimed in, with a knowing look as she popped a donut in her mouth. "Let's just say the latest season of The Collin & Sybil Show isn't exactly a walk in the park."

"Or a pleasant Sunday picnic by the lake," Harmony added with a snort.

I glanced at Finn as he strummed a particularly upbeat tune, and Tabatha twirled around on the dance floor. Her carefree spirit was infectious, and for a brief moment, I imagined what it might be like to let go of all my worries and dance without a care. Except I couldn't dance or handle everyone staring at me. Reality pulled me back like an anchor.

Speaking of being the center of attention and loving every minute of it ...

"Ugh, I was afraid they would be here." I tilted my head toward my father who had just strolled into view, arm-in-arm with Samantha, another vision of perfection.

He looked like a man reborn, wearing that ridiculous plaid shirt I told him would make him look even more like a dad from a sitcom—complete with khakis that were probably intended for a round of golf, but instead paraded around the Harvest Festival. After years of stumbling through the ashes of grief, there I was, the ghost of my mother haunting his every thought.

He was clearly happier without me, yet I missed him terribly.

It was time I faced the facts and accepted that Samantha wasn't going anywhere.

He spotted me from across the sea of festival attendees, his smile wide and unapologetic. "Morti!" he called, his voice booming over the laughter and music, as if he were summoning a reluctant audience member to the stage. "Come say hello to Samantha's family."

Her mother and sister stood behind them, scanning the festival with excitement. The way Samantha leaned into him —her preened hair catching the light like a polished trophy— made my stomach churn. It wasn't just her presence that made my chest tighten—it was everything she represented: change, intrusion, and a future that didn't include me.

"Do I have to?" I muttered under my breath, pinching a piece of donut to keep from expressing my disdain too openly.

My friends glanced at each other, unsure how to navigate this battlefield.

"Think of it as a polite obligation," Byron replied quietly in his calming therapist voice, his eyes telling a different story as they darted between my father's eager wave and my scowling expression.

"Fine." I made my way over to the stage where my father, Samantha, her mother and sister stood talking to

Collin and Sybil. Could things get any more awkward? I should have stayed in bed today.

As I approached, the conversation swirled around me like leaves in the afternoon breeze. My father's laughter rang out, bright and buoyant, a stark contrast to the internal storm brewing within me. Samantha turned, all vibrant energy and practiced charm, her smile stretching wide as if she had just seen a long-lost friend instead of the daughter who felt as though she was disappearing into the backdrop.

"There you are!" My father's voice was buoyant enough to carry across the festival sounds, making me feel like a deer caught in headlights. "Meet Samantha's family —this is her sister, Lila, and her mother, Wilma."

Lila waved, her blonde hair bouncing with every exaggerated gesture. "It's so nice to finally meet you. Sammy has told us so much about you," she said, eyes sparkling with sincerity that made me want to roll my own.

I fought the urge, but drew the line at smiling back. "Nice to meet you as well."

"Morticia," Samantha's mother exclaimed, her voice rich like honey but dripping with expectation. "Samantha has told us so much about you. It is wonderful to finally meet the daughter of our favorite funeral home director."

"My pleasure. Welcome to Mayflower." I shook her manicured hand, mine slightly dry from embalming fluid with short, simple, unpainted nails.

"Sybil was just telling us all about her novel," Lila gushed. "It makes me want to write a thriller."

"I've heard it's not as easy as people think it is," Collin muttered.

"Your father tells me you write poetry," Wilma looked down her nose at me curiously. "How charming." That must be where Samantha got her height from.

"She does much more than that," Collin interjected before I had a chance to speak. "She's amazing at research, and her insights regarding the work of a bestselling thriller author are fascinating. I don't know how she has time to read or write anything with juggling her duties at the funeral home, but if she did write a book of any kind, I would read it for sure."

"Likewise," I said softly, forgetting other people were there until I heard a little gasp and noticed Sybil's jaw fall open, her gaze narrowing as it shifted between Collin and myself.

My father cleared his throat. "Yes, well, *Smith's Funeral Home* couldn't survive without my daughter, that's for sure." He looked me in the eye, and his softened. "Neither could I. She's the glue that holds everything together."

"Thanks, Dad. You give me too much credit." I graced him with my special smile, and he winked. I glanced at my watch. "Well, it was lovely meeting you all, but speaking of work ... I really need to get going." I would say anything at this point to remove myself from this conversation.

"All work and no play?" Collin tilted his head, eyeing me with a look I couldn't quite identify.

"Something like that." I shrugged, waving goodbye and

turning around to walk away before I changed my mind, wondering exactly what game we were playing.

"You work too hard, but don't worry, dear. That's about to change," my father chimed in, freezing me in my tracks.

What did he do? I turned around and eyed him questioningly.

"I know I haven't been much use lately, with my cancer treatments and wedding planning, so I hired you some help." He nodded once.

My stomach bottomed out. "You didn't have to do that. Our team works really well together as is." The thought of someone new invading my comfort zone was not sitting well with me. The funeral home was my safe space.

"Yes, I did. Collin's right. You work far too much. It's not good for your health. The deal is already done. Samantha found him after we posted our help wanted ad."

Him? Of course she did. I inhaled deeply and unclenched my teeth.

"He'll be good for you, honey." Samantha beamed, clearly proud of herself, even though she didn't have a clue what kind of skills were needed to work in a funeral home. "His name is Hank Booker. He's a Jack-of-all-trades, so use him to pick up the slack. Please take care of yourself. We certainly don't need you getting sick again before the wedding."

The only sickness I hoped to have in the near future was morning sickness.

I pasted on a smile and said, "Thank you. How ... thoughtful." Even though a Jack-of-all-trades didn't mean he was qualified to do anything helpful for me. Biting back a sigh, I waved my goodbyes and left before I said something I would regret.

LATER THAT NIGHT, I headed into our funeral home to finish up some work and check on my staff.

Gertrude sat behind the front desk, talking with Beatrice about an upcoming funeral. Eddy and Annette were in the sitting area, going over the plan to get the body ready. Clyde sat at a nearby table, giving a status report on the state of the repairs in the crematory, while Eli went over the maintenance work on the funeral home's current hearse.

A man I had never seen walked in from the back, carrying a toolbox, looking rugged and tough. He was average height, an athletic build, maybe fifty, with a head of thick, wavy brown hair in need of a trim, and a full beard. "The furnace is fixed and filter changed, so you're all set to go when it's cold enough to turn the heat on," he said to Gertrude.

"Oh, bless your heart, Hank. Thank you so much. These old bones of mine don't tolerate the cold too well." Gertrude smiled at him.

"You're a good egg," Beatrice added.

"You must be Hank Booker, our new ... handyman, so to speak." I made my presence known and held out my hand. "I'm Morticia Smith."

Hank wrapped his large hand around mine and smiled at me with kind brown eyes. I was used to refined, but suddenly rugged didn't look too bad. "It's a pleasure to meet you, Ms. Smith. I appreciate you letting me stay on. I'm pretty good at most things. Just say the word, and I'm on it."

The warmth of his palm against mine felt good. Maybe it wouldn't be so bad letting someone new in after all. "Please, call me Morti."

"Morti it is." He finally let go of my hand, as if just realizing he'd held it a little too long.

"Good to finally have a warm set of hands around here." I laughed, trying to mask the lingering uncertainty in my voice. It felt almost surreal to be welcoming new life into the funeral home, smack in the middle of family drama and my own personal crisis.

Gertrude's eyes twinkled with mischief as she leaned towards me. "You'll find Hank is quite handy, Morti. He's already fixed everything from the furnace to my back pain." She shot him a wink that made Hank turn a shade of crimson.

"Just doing what I can," Hank said, his humility disarming. "It's all part of the job."

"Let's hope you don't have to fix too many broken hearts," I murmured, feeling a pang of irony slice through me. After all, I was in the business of mending grief, while my own heart was splintering like brittle branches in winter storms. "So, what's your specialty?" I asked, pushing through my self-doubt, my curiosity keeping me glued to the conversation.

"I can do just about anything—plumbing, electrical work, carpentry," he replied with a relaxed confidence. "But I've also got a knack for fixing things around here that go beyond the physical." He glanced around the room, his eyes lingering on each staff member as if reading their unspoken worries. "Sometimes it's just about talking things out."

I raised an eyebrow. Did he mean he was a handyman or a therapist? I wouldn't put anything past Samantha. Either way, I wasn't sure how much I appreciated being psychoanalyzed in my own domain, especially by a man I barely knew. "You'll find this place is more about the living than the dead," I said lightly, attempting to shield my thoughts behind a veil of humor. "If you can survive our staff, you're golden."

Clyde chortled from his table, his hands weaving together like an old man whittling away at wood. "Good luck with that, Hank. Morti's got a mean streak if you tick her off."

"Do I?" I shot back, feigning indignation while casting a sideways glance at Hank.

His eyes sparkled with mischief, as if he were already plotting ways to keep me on my toes.

"Oh, absolutely." Beatrice leaned in, her voice dripping with sweetness. "You should see her when she's had no coffee and too much paperwork."

"Or during work dinners," Gertrude added with a smirk. "That's when the real fireworks happen."

I crossed my arms defensively. "Speaking of work ..."

"We're just teasing ya, Morti." Eli cleared his throat. "We've got some arrangements to finish, Hank. Morti usually handles the details—she's our very own boss lady, and darn good at it."

I waved off the compliment, uncomfortable with praise. "I prefer to think of myself as the chief procrastinator. But really, Hank, if you're as handy as you say, you'll fit right in."

"Procrastination is just another form of creativity," he countered.

Creativity. Now there was a word I hadn't expected to come from a man like him.

"Creativity?" I echoed, raising an eyebrow. "In a funeral home? The only creative aspect around here is how to get the flowers arranged without triggering someone's allergies."

Hank chuckled, that warm sound wrapping around me like a cozy blanket on a cold night. "Well, Morti, every job has its artistry," he said, gesturing at the freshly polished wooden casket in the corner. "Even that can be an expression of love and memory."

I blinked, caught off-guard by his perspective. Maybe he was more than just a pair of capable hands and a tool belt. "You're not wrong," I admitted slowly, surprised at how easy it was to converse with him, despite my initial reservations. "But let's be real—mostly it's about making sure we don't send someone off in the wrong model."

"I can only imagine." He leaned in closer, lowering his voice conspiratorially as if sharing state secrets. "You know, Morti, I read once that sometimes the best way to tackle overwhelming responsibilities is to prioritize—like sorting through what truly matters first." The intensity of his gaze was a little unnerving. "I can help you with anything you need at work or anywhere else. Just say the word."

I blinked and felt my ears heat. "I say it's been a long day." I raised my voice and stepped back. "Why don't you all call it a night. We'll pick up where we left off tomorrow."

Everyone left and I locked up.

Hank followed me out back with a load of trash he tossed into the dumpster. "Anything else you need before I leave?"

I opened my mouth to speak when Collin appeared from around the side of the building, heading to the door that led to our apartments. He stopped with his hand on the doorknob, glancing between Hank and me.

"I'm all set, Hank. Thanks again for all your help today. I'll see you tomorrow."

Hank nodded once, glanced at Collin, and then headed for his truck in the parking lot.

I walked over to join Collin.

"Who was that?" Collin was the opposite of rugged, but equally as appealing. Except he was dating Sybil. I needed to remember that.

"That was Hank Booker, my new handyman." I smiled and waved to Hank as he pulled out of the parking lot.

Collin frowned. "If you needed help, you should have asked me. You're helping me with research. I would have been happy to return the favor." He shoved his hands in his jeans pockets. "I'm pretty handy."

I shrugged, leaving out the fact that I wasn't the one who hired him. "I wouldn't want to intrude on Sybil's time."

Collin's frown deepened, and I could see the gears turning in his head. "Sybil and I ... we're not exactly on the same page lately." He let out a short, frustrated huff. "It's like trying to read a novel with half the pages missing."

I nodded, unsure how to respond. The tension between us felt heavier, laced with unspoken words. I glanced back at the parking lot, where Hank's taillights blinked away into the night. Why did it feel like the air had thickened around us?

The lines on Collin's forehead carved a furrow so distinct I could practically bury a coffin in it. "Sybil's busy on social media, promoting the book she might never finish," he muttered, the sarcasm draping over the words like damp laundry. "She doesn't talk about anything but herself and her novel. It's getting tiresome. I hope for her fans' sake she comes through and finishes the damn thing."

It turned out Sybil was smarter than I'd ever given her credit for, making me wonder what her end game really was. I couldn't help but feel a twinge of sympathy for him, but I buried it under layers of caution. After all, I had my own problems to navigate—like my father's marriage and the looming reality of impending motherhood via a stranger's sperm.

"Look, Collin," I started, trying to inject a hint of levity into the heavy air between us. "I appreciate the offer of help, really, but I'm all set now that I have Hank."

"So, Hank is the answer to all your problems?" Collin narrowed his eyes, the gray stormier than ever.

"He's the answer to some, yes." I opened the door and headed upstairs with Collin right behind me. When we reached the top, I put my hand on the doorknob to my apartment. "It's been a long day. I'm going to call it a night. Good luck with Sybil."

"So that's it? You're done helping me with my research?"

I looked back at him. "I never said that."

"Then when are you free?" He looked frustrated ... angry almost.

I didn't understand him. He was dating Sybil. What did he want from me? I sighed. "You tell me. You're the one who doesn't seem to have any time."

"I'll make time. No interruptions, I promise." A muscle in his jaw bulged. "Providing you can get away from work."

"I can get away. I just have to plan for it. I'll check my calendar and get back to you on a day and time."

"It's a date." He entered his apartment and gave me one last intense parting look before closing the door.

Chapter Ten

Tonight's girls' night was hosted by Tiffany at the ranch-style house she and Matt bought when she had the twins. Tiffany had high standards, but she didn't cook. Good thing her husband Matt was an excellent cook. He prepared the food, then took the twins over to Zoe and Chaz's house, to hang with Chaz and Byron while Zoe's children entertained the babies. Everyone had that special someone in their lives except me.

Although lately, it seemed as if I'd sparked the interest of two.

Wait until I filled them in on Hottie Handyman Hank and how Confusing Cutie Collin had reacted to that.

I slipped into Tiffany's living room, taking in the string-lights twinkling above like stars trying to make a statement. The scent of roasted vegetables wafted through the air, mingling with laughter that bubbled from the kitchen. Zoe and Harmony were already there, perched on the couch like two enthusiastic birdwatchers spotting a rare species.

"Morti! You made it," Harmony exclaimed, her face lighting up. "We were just debating the merits of beer versus wine versus martinis."

"None. Diet cola would be my choice." I chuckled as I eased onto the couch beside them. "Knowing Tiffany's culinary prowess, I'm guessing we'll need all of them to survive dinner."

"I can't wait to taste what Matt's cooking tonight," Zoe chimed in, her eyes sparkling with mischief. "We might actually get something edible for once—no offense, Tiff." She winked at Tiffany, who was busy rearranging her dish settings on the dining table.

"Hey, I know I have it good, and I thank him every night." Tiffany wagged her brows as she sat beside me, then pulled me into a hug that felt like being enveloped in a cloud of sugar and spice and everything nice. "What's new? Spill all the tea, doll."

I accepted a glass of diet cola and cradled it in my hands. "You wouldn't believe it," I began, careful to keep my voice light despite the swirling emotions that danced beneath the surface. "I've got a new handyman at work, and his name is Hank."

Harmony's eyes widened. "Really? I didn't think I'd ever see the day you hired someone new and let him into your sacred space."

"I didn't hire him. My father let Samantha handle that."

"Oh, boy. She doesn't know the first thing about running a funeral home," Zoe said.

"My thoughts exactly, but he's actually proving to be pretty helpful."

"She *does* know a thing or two about men." Tiffany grinned. "Is he handsome?"

I thought about that. "He certainly isn't ugly. He's like a rugged outdoorsman, with thick wavy hair and a full beard. He's the total opposite of Collin."

"Speaking of Collin, what does he think of Handy Hank?" Harmony sipped her beer.

I leaned back, feeling the plush comfort of the couch envelop me as I recounted the scene from earlier. "They didn't officially meet, but he saw him. He wasn't exactly thrilled," I admitted, biting back a laugh at the memory of Collin's sullen expression. "It felt more like I was discussing a rival than a mere handyman. I don't see why Hank helping me should bother him anyway. He's dating Sybil."

"He's clearly jealous." Tiffany leaned in, her eyes dancing with mischief.

"More like confused," I replied, glancing around the living room to avoid their piercing gazes. "He insists I should have asked him for help instead of hiring Hank. As if I'd want to draw him away from his precious Sybil."

Zoe snickered. "Oh please, Morti. Are you really going to let Sybil stand in the way of something you want?

"Well, no. I just don't know what I want, I guess. For now, I did agree to help Collin with more research. I just have to find time in my schedule. But first, I need your help in picking another sperm donor." I pulled out the book of eligible candidates and set it on the coffee table before us, open to the page of the men I was interested in. "So, which one should I pick for round two?"

The room fell silent, the laughter and chatter evaporating like mist in the morning sun.

"You really want to put yourself through this again?" Harmony eyed me with concern. "You were really upset when it didn't take the first time."

"I'm sure. I'm okay now. I'm being realistic this time, but I am on fertility medication this time, so I do have hope." I fanned my face. "I'm not a fan of the side-effects, though. Hot, cold, laughing, crying ... my emotions are all over the place."

Harmony patted my back, then studied the book.

Zoe leaned forward, her eyes fixed on the page. Her brow furrowed, and I could practically hear the gears clicking in her head as she scanned the candidates.

Meanwhile, Tiffany snatched a handful of chips from the bowl, daintily nibbling on one as she pondered the pages.

"Okay, then, let's see what we're working with," Harmony said, her tone suddenly serious. "This is quite possibly one of the most important decisions of your life, Morti." She handed me a diet cola.

"Thanks for the pressure," I murmured, taking a sip of my soda as if it were one of Harm's magic potions that could ease my nerves.

"Let's start with this guy. It says he's a wilderness guide." Tiffany pointed dramatically at one of the profiles, her nails glinting under the twinkling lights. "He's so rugged, with a perfect smile, and spends his weekends hiking. I bet his boys are strong swimmers."

I rolled my eyes. "Yes, I want it to work this time, but I still have standards. I want a man who's intelligent, at minimum. Not just another pretty face."

"Alright then," Harmony piped up, her finger poised dramatically over the page. "Let's see who we have here. This dude looks like he could star in a toothpaste commercial." She pointed at another handsome man with a bright smile and perfect teeth. "It says he's a dentist. You have to be smart for that, don't you?"

"I would imagine so."

"What about this guy?" Zoe pointed to a dashing man with a stethoscope. "It says he graduated top of his class and is a neurosurgeon."

"Neurosurgeons are the rockstars of the medical world," I mused. "I'm just so torn."

Harmony snorted. "You're overthinking this. Let's focus on these hotties. We need a game plan here." She leaned closer, eyes darting between the profiles like a hawk spotting its prey.

"Okay, fine." I surrendered, flipping through the candidates as if they were glossy magazine pages displaying a lifestyle I could hardly imagine. "Let's look seriously at the ones that don't look like they just walked out of an Abercrombie & Fitch ad."

"Good call," Tiffany said, her finger delicately tracing the spine of one profile that had been cleverly tucked between two others. "What about this one? He's an archaeologist and apparently loves dinosaurs. I mean, you can't go wrong with someone who's passionate about history and has a great sense of humor."

I raised an eyebrow, peering at the man's picture, which featured him wearing a khaki hat that looked suspiciously like it belonged in a Jurassic Park sequel. "Do I want my future child to be fascinated with fossils or to play with blocks? I can't quite decide."

"Why not both?" Harmony chimed in, her enthusiasm unwavering. "Imagine. A tiny Morti, researching fossils during the day and building Lego skyscrapers at night. A true renaissance kid."

"Why not, indeed." I nodded, having a good feeling about my decision. "Ladies, we have a winner." Now if only I could manage my personal life as easily.

It was mid-September before I finally found the time to help Collin with his research regarding the mysterious disappearance on Freedom Lake. It was still warm enough to take a boat out on the water, but just barely. He could have gone himself, but he'd insisted on waiting for me to join him.

Smith's Funeral Home was located on Freedom Lake. We had a rowboat that my father used to take me fishing in, but it hadn't been used in years. I told Collin to meet me out back on the dock.

The early autumn air was crisp and cool, and the leaves on the trees were starting to turn shades of red and orange. The water was calm, reflecting the golden sunlight that filtered through the trees. The rowboat sat at the edge of the dock, its blue paint chipping and its wood weathered from years of neglect.

I made my way over to the water to wait for Collin. The musty scent of old wood from the boat and dock, mixed with the fresh smell of lake water filled the air. The breeze carried the faint scent of fallen leaves and the earthy smell of decaying plants.

The dock was rough and splintered, the wood worn down from years of use. As I made my way onto the rowboat, it rocked slightly on the water, the gentle motion making me feel both nervous and excited.

I looked up and spotted Collin walking my way alone … no Sybil in sight.

His shadow stretched across the dock, a tall silhouette against the vivid colors of the trees. The moment he stepped onto the old wooden planks, it felt as if the world had narrowed down to just the two of us. Collin waved, and I could see his trademark lips tipping up ever so slightly from a smile surfacing beneath the afternoon sun—his full mouth framed by his salt-and-pepper goatee.

I couldn't keep from smiling back just a little.

"Hey, Mona Lisa, nice to see you again," he called out,

his voice playful yet tinged with something deeper, almost conspiratorial. "Ready to dig up some skeletons?"

"Metaphorically or literally?" I shot back, fighting another smile as I tried to mask my rising apprehension.

"Let's keep it metaphorical for now." He stepped onto the boat with ease, unbothered by its wobbling under his weight. "This old thing didn't look half so rickety from shore."

I shrugged, feigning nonchalance. "It's got good bones ... at least that's what my dad always said, but we don't take it out anymore."

"Let me guess ... her name's Wednesday."

"Actually, *his* name is Lurch."

"Well, let's hope he doesn't when we're out in the middle of the lake."

"I think we're safe as long as you don't rock the boat."

Collin laughed, settling himself onto one of the two old wooden seats in the boat. I took my place on the other seat, making sure to distribute our weight evenly.

"Okay, so tell me more about this mysterious disappearance on this here lake," Collin said, his voice taking on a serious tone as he began to row the boat with long smooth strokes as if he'd done so more than once.

"Ah, the tale of the vanishing swan," I replied dramatically, leaning back and crossing my arms as if I was about to recount an ancient legend. "Legend has it that many moons ago, a local woman disappeared while out for a leisurely row on this very lake. They say she was last seen chasing a wayward swan that had strayed too close to the treacherous rocks."

Collin's eyes sparkled with intrigue and something more. "Chasing swans? That's quite the romantic angle."

"Yes, well," I continued, trying to sound more mysterious than I felt. "Some say she was lured into the depths by the lake's siren song, others claim she simply got lost in her own mind and never found her way back."

"Or perhaps the swan was in on it," he mused, his oars splashing rhythmically against the water now. "A conspiracy of nature."

"Her boat was found floating in the center of the lake, and neither she nor the swan were ever seen again. Since then, folks have seen shadows gliding across the water's surface at twilight."

"Sounds like a perfect lead for a horror story," he mused, glancing around warily as he rowed. "But I'm more interested in how it's affected the town. I mean, did it change anything? Any superstitions? Rituals?"

"Superstitions, yes," I answered, tucking behind my ear a strand of hair that had slipped out of my bun as a cool breeze swept through the boat. "People started avoiding the lake after sunset, thinking it might be cursed or something equally dramatic. You know how small towns love their legends."

Collin nodded thoughtfully, his brows knitting together as he focused on rowing, gliding us farther across the lake. The wind picked up, rocking the boat with waves.

"Though, I can't say I blame them," I added, glancing

at the rippling water beneath us. "There's something undeniably eerie about this place when the sun dips below the horizon. Almost like it's holding its breath."

He chuckled softly. "I'd imagine you've got more than a few spooky stories to tell, working at a funeral home and all." His gaze met mine and held.

I felt a flush creep into my cheeks. "Only the best," I replied, crossing my arms defensively. "Like the time someone claimed they saw Aunt Edna's ghost wandering around *Maple Ridge Market* after her funeral. Apparently, she was still trying to find her favorite pie."

"Classic small-town lore." He grinned, glancing out to the horizon where the sun was now a fiery orb sinking into the water. "But in all seriousness, how do you feel about it? The disappearance, I mean. Doesn't it bother you that someone might have met their end here?"

"Oh, sure," I replied with an airy wave of my hand, "but isn't life full of unanswered questions? Like why we insist on putting pineapple on pizza?"

"Right?" He shook his head. "I've never understood the logic behind ruining a perfectly good slice like that."

"The lake has a way of holding onto its secrets," I continued, feeling a sudden thrill at sharing this piece of Mayflower's lore with him. "Sometimes, I wonder if the water remembers every tragedy that's ever occurred here, like an ancient storyteller collecting whispers beneath its surface."

"Or Mother Nature harboring her misbegotten offspring," he added, his voice low and serious, making my heart stutter in surprise. The tension hung thick in the air like the fog creeping over the water.

"Let's hope it's not the latter." I chuckled nervously, attempting to lift the weight of our conversation. "We might just become the next ghost story if we're not careful."

He shot me a sideways glance, his expression curious but unfazed. "It could make for some compelling content. 'The Haunted Rowers of Freedom Lake.'"

"I'll pass, thanks." I wrung my hands. "We'd better turn back. It's getting dark and that fog is growing thicker."

Collin's brow furrowed slightly, and for a moment, I thought I saw a flicker of concern in his eyes, but then he shrugged. "It's just fog. Adds some atmosphere, don't you think? Like a scene from one of Oliver King's thrillers."

"Yeah, but have you ever been out here when it rolls in? It creeps up like something alive, curling around the trees and swallowing the shore whole." I was getting more anxious by the second, my heart racing as shadows lengthened across the water, transforming Freedom Lake into a different kind of beast.

He chuckled again, though this time it was more to reassure me than anything else. "Alright then, let's head back." His oars dipped into the water with renewed urgency as he maneuvered us toward the dock, but even as he picked up speed, I could feel an uninvited chill wriggling its way up my spine.

"Are you trying to drown us?" I exclaimed, gripping the sides of the boat as it bucked beneath us. "Because I'll have you know, I have a very important funeral to attend next week, involving Aunt Edna's infamous pie."

"Okay, okay. I'll ease up," he laughed, moderating his strokes to something less akin to a race. But despite his efforts, the air had thickened around us—alive with an urgency that sent ripples through my thoughts.

I swallowed hard, my eyes darting everywhere at once.

"So tell me," he said casually, steering us back towards the dock while seemingly unaffected by the impending dusk. "What's it like, working at a funeral home every day? I mean, aside from the endless supply of ghost stories."

I hesitated, caught off guard by the sincerity in his question. How to sum up a world cloaked in mourning, yet tangled with the bright threads of life? "It's oddly comforting," I finally admitted, my voice barely above a whisper. "There's a weight to it, sure ... but it also reminds me of how fleeting everything is. Each service is like ... a celebration, really—a way for people to remember and share their stories."

"Celebration of life amidst all that death," he mused, glancing back at me as we neared the dock. "Sounds like an emotional rollercoaster."

I nodded, feeling the familiar tightness in my chest. "You'd be surprised how much laughter can echo in those walls. It's all about perspective." My heart raced at the thought—did he truly understand? Those moments of levity were my lifeline, the glue that held my sanity together amidst the swirling shadows of loss. "In a way," I continued, "it's a constant reminder to embrace the absurdity of living—because honestly, what's more ridiculous than the fact that we all eventually shuffle off this mortal existence while worrying about whether we've remembered to pay the electric bill?"

Collin chuckled, but there was an edge of understanding in his laughter—a shared acknowledgment of life's quirks that felt almost electric. As the boat bumped softly against the wooden dock, his gaze lingered on me for a moment too long, as if he were weighing his words carefully.

"You have an interesting perspective on mortality, Morti," he said, finally lifting his oars and setting them down. The sudden stillness hung between us like a drawn curtain, and I could feel my heart thumping loudly in my chest.

"Interesting? You mean morbid?" I replied, half-joking to lighten the moment.

His gaze lingered on the horizon then held mine steady. "I can only picture the antics. But it also sounds ... lonely?"

There it was again—the prickly truth. "Lonely is one way to put it," I replied, feeling exposed under his scrutiny. "But there's something to be said for solitude, too. Like a canvas waiting for color."

"Morti, I—"

"There you are, Collin." Sybil waved from the shoreline. "I almost called Officer Pickles, you were gone so long. That lake is dangerous, you know."

"We weren't gone that long, but here I am, safe and

sound," he called back, as he stepped out of the boat, reaching down to help me out.

I took his hand and stepped onto the dock, letting go before I did something stupid like pull him in for a hug.

"Thanks for the history lesson, Morti. What are your plans for the evening?"

I held up my hands. "It's a mystery."

"I always loved a good mystery." He winked.

My heart gave a little flutter.

"Collin, come on. It's cold out here," Sybil called from the shoreline.

Collin sighed. "Duty calls."

The sound of the dumpster rattling drew our attention. Hank tossed a second bag of trash in and then waved to me, giving a slight head nod to Collin with watchful eyes.

I waved back to Hank, gracing him with a smile, and then shrugged at Collin. "I guess duty calls for me, too." I walked past him and Sybil, my steps suddenly lighter.

Chapter Eleven

It was late September now. Mayflower was gearing up for the Leaf Peepers who came out in droves during the month of October to view the fall foliage. It was great for the town's restaurants and businesses, but annoying for its residents. People would block side roads and driveways, trying to get the perfect shot.

I drove to *Ginger's Greenhouse* to get some mums, bales of hay, cornstalks, and pumpkins to spruce up the outside of the funeral home. Hank had taken over keeping up the grounds, as well as many other odds and ends. He was a man of many talents, and kept surprising me every day, like when I caught him reading a book on his lunch break.

There was more to him than I had realized, and I was intrigued ... and confused.

Hank was single and interesting, while Collin was taken ... yet I couldn't stop thinking about Collin. Why did

I always want what I couldn't have? I couldn't take any more of Sybil's silly giggles throughout the house. I could hear her over at Collin's apartment. The funeral home was ancient, and sound traveled through the registers. There was no escaping it.

So I made my excuses and left for a much-needed break.

I parked Fester in the parking lot out back and headed inside the greenhouse, only to run into Samantha. She was perusing bulbs to plant for spring blooms. She hadn't seen me yet, so I turned around to head back outside.

Too late.

"Morticia, wait," she said from behind me.

I pasted on a smile and turned back around. "Samantha, nice to see you. What's going on?"

"Oh, I'm just getting a head start on my spring garden." She eyed me suspiciously. "What are you doing here?"

"I'm picking up some fall decorations for the funeral home."

"Why didn't you have Hank do that?" She tossed up her hands, clearly frustrated. "He's there to help you with these sorts of things, to lighten your load. Is he not working out? Because I can hire someone else if you'd like."

"No, no. Hank has been great. Thank you. I just needed some air."

"Ahhh," she looked at me with knowing eyes, "is it Collin Quinn?"

I blinked.

"Honey, everyone can see the sparks that fly between you two."

"It doesn't matter. Sybil is a human fire extinguisher. As long as she's around, I don't stand a chance, so I'm moving on.

Her eyes widened. "With Hank?"

"No ... maybe ... I don't know." I shook my head. "I'm beginning to think romance is overrated. I just want a family of my own."

Her eyes softened. "I understand that more than you know."

I sucked in a breath as my biggest fear was presenting itself. "So you, um, and my father ..."

"Well, me anyway. I haven't exactly convinced him yet." She winked.

I frowned. "I get why *you* want a child. You don't have any children yet. But my father has me. That might be enough for him." I shrugged. "Maybe that's something you should consider."

Her smiled slipped. "I'm not trying to take your father away from you or replace you with another baby. Why can't he have both? *We* are your family, Morti. Maybe that is something *you* should consider." Leaving her bulbs behind, she spun on her heel and left the greenhouse, clearly upset with me again.

I sighed.

I didn't mean to sound so bitchy—I just didn't like change. My father was *mine*, and I wasn't ready to share him. It was selfish. I knew that. I wanted him to be happy, but why couldn't he be happy with a woman his age? Someone who was ready to retire and travel the world and go on adventures. Not someone who wanted to have his baby ...

Especially after everything he'd been through with my mother.

No longer in the mood to shop, I headed outside to the parking lot to go home. I had nearly reached Fester when I stopped short. Someone had slashed my tires. I walked around the hearse to confirm that all four were slashed. Chills crept up my spine and I spun around, feeling like someone's gaze was burning a hole in my back.

Ever since Collin had told me he'd felt like someone was watching him, following him, I kept having the same feeling. I scanned the parking lot but didn't see anyone, so I pulled out my phone and dialed a number.

"Officer Pickles here."

"Don!" I blurted, my heart pounding.

"Morticia Smith? Is that you? What's wrong?"

"I'm at *Ginger's Greenhouse*. Someone just slashed all my tires."

"Are you in danger? Go inside."

"No, no. The parking lot is empty. Whoever it was is long gone."

"Stay put. I'll be right there."

I leaned against my hearse, trying to calm my racing heart. I had always been a bit paranoid, but ever since Collin had mentioned feeling like someone was watching him, I couldn't shake the feeling that I was being followed as well.

As I waited for Officer Pickles to arrive, I pulled out my phone and called Hank.

"Hey Morti, what's going on?" His voice sounded concerned.

I took a deep breath to stop from shaking. "Someone slashed all four of my tires."

"What? Are you alright? Do you need me to come down there?"

"It's okay. Don is on his way."

"Don?"

"Sorry, Officer Pickles. We went to high school together."

"Gotcha."

"Can you let the funeral home staff know what happened? I won't be able to make it back anytime soon."

"Of course. Do you want me to come over later and help change your tires?"

"I'm not sure how I'm handling this yet, but I'll keep you posted."

As we hung up, Don pulled into the parking lot with sirens blaring. He quickly parked his patrol car and hopped out.

"Morticia, are you alright?" He adjusted his hat and dropped his hands to his hips, studying me. "Should I call Dr. Joy?"

I was already shaking my head. "I'm fine. Just a little shaken up."

He nodded and looked over at my slashed tires. "Do you have any idea who would do something like this?"

I shook my head. "No. But I think someone might be following me. And Collin mentioned feeling the same way since he's been in town."

Don's eyebrows shot up in surprise. "Collin Quinn? The new travel writer in town renting your dad's place?"

"Yes." I frowned. "Do you think this could be connected?"

He rubbed his chin thoughtfully before responding. "It's hard to say for sure without any evidence or leads, but it's definitely worth looking into." He pulled out a notepad and pen from his pocket and started taking notes.

After we finished talking and I assured him I didn't need a tow, Don left to continue his investigation. I texted Hank and asked him to bring the spare tires we had in the garage so we could change them in the parking lot. We always kept spare tires on hand for emergencies, given we couldn't afford for our hearse to break down during a funeral procession to the cemetery. Since I drove our old hearse, I knew the tires would fit.

Hank arrived in minutes. As we were changing the tires, he spoke with an edge to his voice. "Morti, I don't want to alarm you, but I think someone has been watching your place, too."

I paused, my hands still gripping the wrench. "What? How do you know?"

"I caught a glimpse of someone in the trees behind the funeral home yesterday. I thought it was just my imagination until I saw them again today," he confessed, glancing over his shoulder as if expecting to see an ominous shadow. "I've seen a figure lurking around the funeral home late at night as well, when I stay behind to organize things."

My heart sank further at his words, the weight of our shared paranoia settling heavily in my chest. "You're serious?"

"Yeah, I mean, it's probably nothing," he rushed to add, glancing up at me with his warm brown eyes that were now clouded with concern. "But I can't shake the feeling that there's more to this story."

I took a deep breath, my mind racing through a thousand scenarios. "What did they look like?"

Hank shrugged, tightening the last bolt on another spare tire. "I didn't get a good look—just a glimpse really. But it felt ... off." He paused for a moment, gnawing his lip. "It's probably just some kid messing around. You know how small towns are."

"Yeah, kids with knives in parking lots." My voice came out sharper than intended, but my nerves were fried.

"Did I hear you tell Gertrude at work that Collin guy is being followed, too?"

I nodded. "I guess we're both being stalked." I shoved another bolt onto another tire, the metallic clank echoing in the tense air between us.

"Have you told Collin about this incident today?" He studied me with a troubled gaze.

"No. Sybil is over at his place." I shrugged, which was half the reason I'd left. "I didn't want to bother him."

"Good." Hank hesitated. "How well do you know Collin?"

I wrinkled my brow. "In person, not very long. But I've known him online for years in *The King's Quills*."

Hank quirked a brow. "Is that one of those reading groups you recommended to me when you saw me reading the other day?"

I nodded absently, still processing everything that had just happened.

"I thought you said you just joined that group after Collin recommended it to you." Hank arched a brow. "He hasn't been in town that long, has he?"

Crap. "I mean, it's *felt* like years that I've known him, especially since I'm helping him with his research. We're both Oliver King fans."

"Oliver King, huh." He looked back at the tire.

"Yes. He's an amazing thriller writer. You should give him a try."

Hank grunted. "Dramas are more my thing." He stood and stored the last of the bolts and tools back in his toolbox.

"Thank you." I smiled and held out my hand. "I, for one, have had enough drama to last me a lifetime."

He wrapped his large hand around my much smaller one, his warm brown eyes softening. "My pleasure." His face turned serious. "I don't like you alone in that house."

"I'm not alone, remember? I have Collin."

He ignored that, dropping my hand. "You need any more help, just give me a ring, day or night. I mean that."

I nodded and then climbed into Fester, shutting and

locking the door before driving away. Glancing in my rear-view mirror, I watched Hank just stand there, solid and strong, staring after me. It was nice to know I could count on someone.

LATER THAT EVENING as dusk settled over the funeral home, I sent everyone home and locked up. I'd been so late for work earlier, that I had left the slashed tires in the back of the hearse. Deciding to store them in the garage until I had time to dispose of them and buy four new spares, I headed out back to Fester.

Unlocking the trunk, I started hauling them out one by one and setting them on the ground. More like dropping them because they were so heavy. More chill bumps popped out on my arms when I spotted a shadow in the dark, just like Hank had said. Gripping a tire iron in my hand, I closed the doors to the trunk and stepped back.

"Show yourself, right now!" I shouted.

"Morti? What's gotten into you?" Collin stepped into the light, the silver at his temples glowing. The rest of his black, slicked-back hair was a little messy ... so unlike him.

How well do you know him ...

I blinked, smothering Hank's words echoing in my head, chalking them up to jealousy. "Collin, you scared me."

He shrugged, shoving his hands in his pockets. "Sorry. Sybil and I got into a fight. She left and I went for a walk."

He scrubbed a hand over his salt-and-pepper goatee. "Why are you so jumpy?"

"Someone slashed my tires at the greenhouse."

His forehead wrinkled and he stepped closer to me, his intense gray gaze inspecting every inch of me. "Are you hurt? Why didn't you call me?"

"You were busy with Sybil. I didn't want to bother you."

Collin frowned. "You're not a bother, Morti. I'm never too busy for you."

"It's okay." I crossed my arms over my mid-section. "I called Hank."

Collin's frown turned to a scowl. "Handyman Hank to the rescue again," he muttered under his breath, but I heard him. His face softened when he looked at me. "I'm sorry, Morti. I should have been here for you."

"It's fine." I looked back at the tires, feeling a sense of unease wash over me.

"Did you see who did it?" Collin asked, stepping closer to the tires.

I shook my head. "No, but I felt a presence."

His sleek black brows furrowed in concern. "Do you think it's connected to whoever is following me?"

"I don't know, but it does seem too coincidental that we're both being targeted," I replied, feeling a shiver run down my spine.

"I didn't want to alarm you," his gaze locked onto mine, "but there was a dead rat in my apartment earlier."

My jaw unhinged as my stomach flipped. "I know this house is old, but I can assure you we don't have rats."

"I'm not saying you do. I'm pretty sure my stalker left me a present. On a platter. On my kitchen table, with silverware and a napkin no less. Maybe we should talk to the police," Collin suggested, reaching out to rest a hand on my shoulder.

I nodded, grateful for his support. "Officer Pickles is investigating my tire-slashing. We can talk to him about this latest news together tomorrow."

"Sounds like a plan." He looked down at the tires. "In the meantime, how can I help?"

We worked together to load the tires into the garage and then made our way back to the funeral home. As we started to open the door to the stairwell leading up to our apartments, I couldn't shake off the feeling of being watched again.

"Do you feel that?" I whispered to Collin.

He stopped and turned around to look at me. "Feel what?"

"I feel like someone is watching us right this minute," I said nervously.

Collin glanced around the yard, his gaze narrowed and intense, before placing a comforting hand on my back this time. "It's probably just your nerves getting to you. Let's get some rest and deal with this in the morning."

I nodded in agreement as we stepped inside the stairwell, then I locked the door, turning the deadbolt. When we reached the top of the stairs, I headed to my apartment, and he walked over to his.

As I unlocked my door, I looked over my shoulder. "I'm glad you're here, neighbor."

He nodded once. "Me, too. Let's see about updating your security system tomorrow, too. You never can be too careful."

"If I didn't know any better, I'd swear we were in the middle of an Oliver King novel." I laughed.

"No kidding," he chuckled, "but I can tell you one thing. I'm not about to live through one of his endings."

"Amen to that." I shuddered. "'Night, Collin."

"'Night, Morticia."

I stepped inside and closed the door, leaning back against it as a thought kept circling in my brain. *An Oliver King novel* ... Slashed tires, stalkers, a dead rat. I sucked in a sharp breath as one certainty became crystal clear.

I'd seen this before!

Chapter Twelve

After staying up most of the night, going over every Oliver King novel I owned—which was all of them —I tossed and turned, then gave up on sleep. In the wee hours of the morning, I put on a pot of coffee, donned a black silk robe over the two-piece skull-and-bones pajama set the girls had gotten me for Christmas, and then crossed the hall. Knocking on Collin's door, I stepped back and crossed my arms, tapping my fuzzy coffin slipper impatiently.

Several minutes later, a sleepy-eyed Collin opened the door. My lips parted. He wore charcoal-gray silk bottoms that looked to be part of a set as well, but the top was missing. I blinked, staring at his bare, sculpted torso with a light sprinkling of hair covering his muscled chest.

"Morti, is something wrong?" He ran a hand over his messy hair and stared at me with a confused gaze.

"No ... yes ... I don't know."

"Well, that's helpful." He chuckled. "Do you know what time it is? The sun isn't up yet."

"I know. I couldn't sleep. I found something. Come with me." I grabbed his arm, then thought better of it. "After you put on a shirt that is."

He looked down as if just realizing he was half naked. "Be right back." Minutes later, he joined me with the matching pajama shirt in place and buttoned, thank the Lord. He'd donned a pair of moccasin slippers as well. "Please tell me there's coffee. I know you don't drink any."

Unlike me, who'd been up all night, he looked as if he'd slept like the dearly departed in the morgue beneath us.

"I keep some on hand just for you ... and my father, of course."

"Of course." He followed me without another word, but I'd seen the small smile tip up one side of his mouth.

I led the way into my apartment, heading straight to the kitchen and pouring him a big cup of black coffee. Then I proceeded to make a large mug of hot white chocolate for myself. I set our cups on my kitchen table, then went to my bookshelf and pulled out a novel. Returning to the table, I set the book in front of Collin.

He blinked. "An Oliver King book?"

"Not just any Oliver King book. This is *Veil of Secrets*. The very first book in *The Shadow Files* series that made him a huge success."

"You have his first book?" He looked at me in surprise. "That's so old."

"It's a classic." I winked. "I have *all* of his books."

"Wow."

"Told you, I am a superfan."

"I guess so." His forehead wrinkled. "But how is this crack-of-dawn-worthy news?"

"The dead rat." I watched his face. "The slashed tires ..."

His eyes widened. "You think whoever is stalking us is copying King's book?"

I shrugged. "I'm not sure. I mean, we're both superfans of King. Maybe this person is trying to send a message, but I'm not sure what."

"You might be onto something. If I remember correctly, in this book, someone is stalking Detective Gideon Wolfe's girlfriend."

"That's right, and genius reporter Serena Blackwood unravels the mystery. The perpetrator was someone Wolfe had put in jail, taking him away from his love."

Collin nodded. "So, the killer enacted his revenge through taking away Gideon's love by killing her."

"But not before toying with them both by leaving the dead rat for him and slashing her tires." I flipped my long hair over my shoulder. "I don't get it. In the book, the perpetrator went after Wolfe's greatest desire. Sybil is your girlfriend, not me. So why am I being the one targeted?"

His gaze met mine and held. "Maybe the perpetrator knows me better than I know myself?"

"Or maybe we're making more out of this than there is." I looked away and took a sip of my hot chocolate, not ready to go there. "So, how's Sybil? Did you two make up?"

Collin's expression shifted, a shadow crossing his features. "We talked, but it didn't go as I'd hoped. It seems like she's been ... different lately."

"Different how?" I leaned forward, the intrigue bubbling up inside me like Tiffany's Champagne.

He ran a hand through his slick hair, visibly agitated. "More obsessed with being the perfect girlfriend in public. You'd think she's trying to fit into some mold that doesn't really exist. It feels forced."

I nodded slowly. "Like she's trying to be more of who she thinks you want, rather than just being herself?"

"Exactly." He sighed, taking a sip of coffee and grimacing slightly at the heat. "It's like I've lost the girl I fell for online, and now I'm stuck with a caricature of her. It just doesn't add up how she can be so different in person."

I couldn't help but feel a pang of sympathy mixed with guilt. "That must be tough," I said quietly. "You deserve someone authentic."

"Right? And then there's you," he said, his voice low and almost hesitant. "She doesn't like you helping me with my research, and she especially won't like us collaborating on trying to figure out who this stalker is." His gaze met mine. "You're handling this situation like a pro, by the way. I could learn a thing or two from you."

I snorted, waving my hand dismissively. "Oh please, if my life were an Oliver King novel, I'd be the tragic side character who gets eaten by the villain early on." I didn't do well with compliments. "If anything, we both seem to be stuck in a very messy subplot. You're the brooding hero with a complicated love life, while I'm ... I'm just Morti Smith, the girl who spends too much time thinking about death and reading thrillers." I sighed. "Here I am, standing in the spotlight of my own horror story, while you have a front-row seat to my impending doom."

Collin shook his head, a smile tugging at the corner of his lips. "You're not going anywhere, Morti. If anyone's going to get eaten, it'll be me trying to protect you. I'm more like the bumbling sidekick who trips over his own feet."

"More like the handsome hero," I said, blinking over my rambling, but I couldn't seem to stop myself. "I mean, we could add some romantic subplots like King's newer books, if you want—daring escapades and unexpected twists."

He leaned back in his chair, crossing his arms with an amused expression. "So, we're writing our own narrative now?"

"Yes! Let's do it. Let's write a book together."

He chuckled. "I tried that once. Years ago. It didn't work out so well."

"Really?" My eyes widened, impressed. "You wrote a novel?"

He nodded. "An old college buddy of mine, Hector Baldwin, was in my English Literature class. We wrote a mystery together, but it was terrible." He laughed, shaking his head. "It never sold, thank God. Some things should never see the light of day."

"Ah, but you didn't write a book with *me*. That would be award winning for sure." I wagged my brows, enjoying our banter. "Front page of Funeral Home Digest."

Collin chuckled softly. "You keep surprising me, Morticia Smith. You have a quick wit and smarts. You think of things critically; you analyze every detail. It's kind of what makes you good at what you do."

I raised an eyebrow, caught off guard by his compliment. "Are we talking about the funeral home business or being a King wannabe?"

"Both," he said earnestly. "You look for clues in everything around you. Like how you figured out this stalker might be mimicking King's work."

"I just have a dark imagination." I shrugged, trying to downplay my enthusiasm about being recognized for something—anything.

"Dark imagination or not, it's a gift." He leaned in closer, an odd expression settling over his chiseled face. "And I think it's time we put those skills to work."

I felt a shiver of excitement mixed with trepidation run down my spine. "What do you mean?"

"We need to investigate this stalker further. If they're echoing King's plotlines, there might be clues hidden in plain sight," Collin suggested, his voice a low murmur. "We could start by keeping an eye out for anything unusual in the neighborhood, maybe even speak to some of the locals."

"Like interviewing my neighbors and grocery store clerks? That sounds ... fun," I replied sarcastically, but underneath it all, I felt a rush of adrenaline—a thrill that made my heart race. I hadn't had this much excitement in my life since high school.

"Exactly! We'll be like a quirky detective duo, taking on the sinister forces of Mayflower," he said, grinning wide enough to momentarily lighten the situation.

"Maybe." I laughed, then noticed the time. "But first, the day job calls." I stood and put our cups in the sink. "Sorry for getting you up so early. I had to stop myself from pounding on your door in the middle of the night."

"I don't mind. You can knock on my door any time." He stood and followed me to my door so I could let him out. "I have to compile my research and start my article anyway. Thanks for the coffee."

"You're welcome." I bit my bottom lip. "And, um, feel free to knock on my door any time as well."

"Careful what you wish for, neighbor." He winked and then disappeared inside his apartment, closing the door behind him.

His door might be closed ... but was that an opening to his heart?

It was early October, and I'd woken up with cramps and my period. Another failed attempt at getting pregnant. I blinked back tears, reminding myself that I knew this was a possibility. I'd failed at my first attempt on my own, but I'd had such hope with having Dr. Joy do the insemination process the second time around. Inhaling a deep breath, I refused to let this be the end of my journey.

I was determined to make the third time the charm.

This time I didn't seek help from the girls or anyone else. I flipped through the book of donors, closed my eyes, and pressed my finger down on an open page. The man was an actor, extremely outgoing, pale skinned and blue eyes ... not my usual type at all. But so far, the way I'd chosen a donor hadn't worked.

Throwing caution to the wind, I chose my candidate and didn't look back.

In the meantime, I planned to focus on catching this stalker. Who better to help with Oliver King trivia than the fans who knew him best? I set my ice cream bowl in my sink, then curled up on my couch and opened my laptop, logging into *The King's Quills*.

Morticia Smith: *Hi everyone. Collin and I need your help. I normally wouldn't ask, but this is Oliver King related, I promise.*

Collin Quinn: *Oh, I didn't realize we were taking this to the group, Morti, but that's not a bad idea.*

Stacy Rose: *My goodness, what kind of plot twist is happening?*

She Wolf: *I have to say you've certainly hooked my interest.*

I filled the group in on the stalking, tire-slashing, and dead rat on the dinner table. Then I told them about my suspicions regarding an Oliver King copycat, reenacting the *Veil of Secrets novel.*

Captain Rogers: *Well, there, matey, I'll keep a lookout on the cyber horizon for possible clues and let you know if I spot any scallywags headed your way.*

Tie Dye Dotty: *Wasn't that King's first novel? I barely remember that one.*

Hans Brewmeister: *It was overrated, in my opinion.*

Collin Quinn: *Overrated? It had to have some merit, because it launched his career.*

Morticia Smith: *I agree, it wasn't my favorite book of his, but no one can deny The Shadow Files series certainly put King on the map.*

Marky Mouse: *Didn't Gideon Wolfe's girlfriend get kidnapped in that one?*

Collin Quinn: *Exactly! And that's what makes this so intriguing. If someone is reenacting the plot, we might just be able to connect the dots.*

Morticia Smith: *Yes! And the twist was that it was the town's parcel-delivery man, but Detective Wolfe put him away years ago for robbing all the local businesses, so he killed Wolfe's girlfriend out of revenge when he got out.*

She Wolf: *Oh, you guys are getting me all wound up about my favorite plots. I live for this. That's when genius reporter Serena Blackwood uncovered a lead that led to the delivery man's arrest.*

Stacy Rose: *That's also when the attraction started between Gideon and Serena. I just love their chemistry.*

Hans Brewmeister: *Of course you do. I personally am all about the plot. I could do without the romance angle.*

Captain Rogers: *Romance makes the world go round, my boy. They make good mates for sure. That gets me thinking, what if the stalker is someone you least expect? Don't trust anyone, not even your closest mates!*

Collin Quinn: *You really think it could be a local? That would be a chilling revelation.*

Morticia Smith: *It's possible. If they're mimicking King, they might think they're some kind of twisted hero in their own story. But we also just had the harvest festival and have the leaf peepers coming next week. It could very well be a stranger passing through, but the King connection makes me think it's something personal.*

Tie Dye Dotty: *Maybe they're trying to send you a message, Morti? You are the Queen of Cadavers, after all.*

Marky Mouse: *Or Collin. Maybe someone followed him to Mayflower. You both are King fans. There has to be a connection somehow.*

Morticia Smith: *I'm not sure what kind of a message they're sending when it involves slashing your tires or getting a dead rat as an invitation. Invitation to what ... murder?*

She Wolf: *Maybe it's someone trying to impress you or Collin with their "passion" for King's work. You know how twisted fans can be.*

Captain Rogers: *Aye, matey. Some landlubbers have strange ways of showing their affection.*

Hans Brewmeister: *Or their animosity. Like you said, Captain, I wouldn't trust anyone.*

Collin Quinn: *Let's not jump to conclusions just yet.*

We need to gather more intel. If we truly suspect someone in Mayflower is behind this, we can't stir the pot too much. It could drive them underground.

Morticia Smith: *Right. Subtlety might be key here.*

I stared at the screen, a chill creeping up my spine. What if this stalker really was targeting us? I could almost hear the dramatic music playing in the background, a fitting score for our impending doom.

Collin Quinn: *Whoever it is, it sounds like they have an unhealthy obsession with Oliver King, and we just happen to be unlucky collateral damage in their twisted narrative.*

Morticia Smith: *Great. Just what I need—an obsessed fan who thinks they're writing their own bestseller through our misery. I've got enough drama unfolding in my life without adding 'potential murder victim' to my résumé.*

Stacy Rose: *You definitely need to be on your guard. It's time to channel your inner Serena Blackwood!*

She Wolf: *And Collin can be Gideon Wolfe! You're both so smart, I'm sure you can get to the bottom of this.*

Collin Quinn: *I'm game if you are, Morti.*

Morticia Smith: *Count me in, but what about Sybil? Aren't you helping her with her book?*

Collin Quinn: *You let me worry about her.*

Hans Brewmeister: *Good luck with that.*

Stacy Rose: *You know where we are if you need us.*

Morticia Smith: *Thank you all for your support. Stay tuned ...*

Chapter Thirteen

I t was mid-October, and the leaf peepers had shown up in droves to see the brilliant fall colors. I needed to clear my head, so I donned my coat and went for a walk. The trees along Lighthouse Lane were a riot of oranges, reds, and yellows, making it look like a painting come to life, and the rolling hills in the distance were breathtaking.

The sidewalks were bustling with tourists, cameras in hand, capturing the stunning fall foliage. The air was crisp and cool, carrying scents of apple cider and pumpkin spice from the nearby cafes and bakeries, mingling with the earthy smell of fallen leaves.

As I passed by a street vendor, the aroma of freshly baked apple pies and warm maple syrup drifted my way, making my mouth water. The gentle rustle of leaves and cheerful chatter of tourists filled the air, punctuated by the occasional honking of car horns. The cool breeze sent a shiver down my spine, making me hug my coat tightly around me, reminding me I wasn't alone.

Someone was always watching me.

Collin and I had been spending a lot of time together, focusing on who might be stalking us. He had all the research he needed for his article on small towns, so when he wasn't investigating with me, he was writing.

Sybil didn't like that one bit.

The only reason I had free time to do anything was because Hank had been a godsend, picking up the slack on whatever I needed at the funeral home. If only he could plan my father's bachelor party, I'd be golden.

My father was a man of simple tastes. He didn't really have any hobbies, or anything special he was into, so I had no idea what kind of party he might like. Zoe was a party planner, but my father didn't want anything fussy, and his fiancé Samantha insisted I do my part and plan the party myself.

Hence the need for a walk to clear my head.

As I strolled through the picturesque streets of Mayflower, my thoughts fought for dominance—tangled threads of anxiety and impending doom, woven with the mundane worries of planning a bachelor party. The scent of freshly baked goods wafted past me again, prompting my stomach to growl in protest.

Maybe a slice of pie would ground me before I dove headfirst into the clues. But as I turned the corner, my heart plummeted. There it was ... a familiar figure wearing a bright-red hat near the entrance of *Pilgrim Perks Cafe*.

Sybil.

Her eyes locked onto mine, and an unsettling wave of dread washed over me as I recalled our last encounter, filled with thinly veiled jealousy and biting remarks.

"Morti!" she called, her voice sweet as saccharin but laced with undertones that made my skin prickle. "What a lovely day for a walk. Care for some coffee?"

I forced a smile, my mind racing with thoughts of Collin and the investigation we were entangled in. A casual coffee with Sybil felt like inviting a tornado into my already frazzled life. "Oh, just out for some fresh air," I replied, my voice barely above a whisper, as if too much volume would alert the nearby tourists of our brewing storm.

"Fresh air? Or running away from something?" Her smile widened, but her eyes glimmered like daggers.

She was a gifted actress, that was for sure. One moment, she played an innocent, naïve woman who made people fall for her charms. The next, she was an intelligent, cunning vixen who would stop at nothing to get what she wanted. She was up to something for sure.

"Just needed to think," I managed, trying to sidestep the trap she was laying. The last thing I wanted was for her to sense any weakness in me—a chink in my armor that could be exploited.

"Well, you do look like you have a lot on your mind," she chirped, tilting her head as if examining a two-headed woman at a carnival. "I hope it's not too heavy. I hear the café has the best pumpkin spice lattes this side of the coast."

"I was actually thinking about grabbing a piece of pie. You know—fuel for planning Dad's bachelor party." I shifted from foot to foot, feeling so awkward.

"Right, the bachelor party." Her smile didn't quite reach her eyes. "That must be quite the undertaking. I don't know how you have time to do anything else."

"I manage." I shrugged. "Hank's a big help."

"Lucky you, to have such an attentive man in your life." She studied me closely.

"Yes, Hank is a great *assistant*." I kept my gaze locked on her, refusing to let her get the upper hand. "All my employees are very attentive. Makes my job much easier, so I can focus on other important things going on in my life at the moment." Like Collin's research and figuring out who our stalker is I left unsaid.

"I'm sure your father is your top priority." *Or should be* was implied by her tone. "I can't imagine your father wanting anything too extravagant."

The word "extravagant" rolled off her tongue like a threat wrapped in silk. My instincts screamed at me to dodge the coffee invitation and keep walking, but the ever-present dread of confrontation coiled tightly around my chest.

"Yeah, simple is definitely his style," I said, forcing enthusiasm into my voice as if it could mask the tension.

Sybil's smile widened, her cheeks stretched tight. "I would love to help. I have some fabulous suggestions for a low-key, yet unforgettable bachelor party. You know, something that really celebrates your father's new chapter without making it feel too ..." she paused dramatically, her eyes narrowing, "overwhelming."

I resisted the urge to roll my eyes. Was she really trying to paint herself as the magnanimous party planner, out to save the day? Or was she out to make a fool of me? "Thanks, but I think I'll stick to my usual flair for simplicity," I replied, feigning a chipper tone that didn't quite make it to my eyes.

"Of course." Sybil's voice dripped with sweet condescension. "A woman of classic taste, right? But you might want to sprinkle in some excitement—just a dash of pizzazz could make all the difference." Sybil's lips curled into a smirk, the kind that made me feel as though she was savoring a secret I wasn't privy to. "After all, what's a good party without a touch of flair?" Her tone was syrupy, but her eyes glinted with something sharper.

"Flair, right." I forced a laugh that sounded more like a strangled croak. "I'll keep that in mind."

Talk about mixing oil and water.

Just then, a couple of tourists wandered by, snapping selfies with the vibrant autumn leaves as their backdrop. They looked blissfully unaware of the brewing storm between us. I envied them.

"Maybe we could brainstorm over that coffee?" Sybil pressed, gliding closer like a shark circling its prey. "What do you say?"

"Oh, I don't know. If I need help, I have Zoe. Besides, I'm kind of a solo act—"

She cut me off, ignoring any notion of me refusing her. "After all, a well-planned event can really bring people together, don't you think?" She leaned in slightly, reminiscent of a cat about to pounce on an unsuspecting mouse. "Especially when it comes to celebrating love." She sighed dreamily, hinting that she was in love as well.

"Right, *love*," I echoed, my stomach turning sour. "But really, it's my father's day. I just want something low-key."

"Low-key but memorable," Sybil interjected brightly, oblivious—or perhaps perfectly aware—of the tension curling around us like smoke from a dying candle. The woman was relentless. "How about a small gathering at McGinny's? They have those charming beer flights and hearty Irish stew. It could feel so festive, and maybe Samantha's sister will combine the bachelorette party, so you don't have to be two places at once." Her eyes hardened slightly. "I mean, you're in such demand these days. It has to be exhausting."

It was as if she had taken all my late-night anxieties and laid them bare before both of us. "In demand," I repeated, forcing a chuckle that felt more like a choke. "Yes, well, it's all about time management."

"Time management," she repeated, with a mocking tilt of her head. "When do you think you'll leave room for some fun? You know, after being the dutiful daughter and all." A smirk danced on her lips, and I could practically hear the clock ticking away my sanity.

I took a step back, distancing myself from her suffocating aura. "Fun is overrated," I declared, attempting to reclaim some bizarre sense of control over this crazy conversation. "Not everything has to be a spectacle."

"Maybe that's where you're mistaken." She leaned in closer, her voice dropping to conspiratorial tones that sent ice through my veins. "Spectacles can be thrilling, Morti."

The way she said *thrilling* had me suddenly wondering if she could be the person behind the pranks against Collin and me. She was jealous of us working together, and she knew we both loved Oliver King novels. She also had access to his apartment and Fester.

I cleared my throat. "I think I've had enough thrills to last me a lifetime lately." I glanced at my watch. "Thanks for the party tips, but I'll have to pass on coffee. I really have to head back to the funeral home. Duty calls." I spun around and headed back home at a fast pace, not giving her a chance to reply, but that didn't stop the daggers of her gaze from piercing my back and sending chills of impending doom down my spine.

"THERE YOU ARE," my father said, charging out the front door of our funeral home when I hit the driveway.

"I went for a walk. What's wrong?" I met him just outside the doors.

"Eddy and Annette were down in the morgue preparing Petunia Pepperdine's body. As the oldest resident of Mayflower, her funeral is a town event. She was one-hundred-and-ten years old and had outlived most of her family. Mayor Edwards has big plans that don't involve a cremation." My father mopped his forehead, looking stressed.

"I know all of this already, Dad. What are you talking about?" Maybe his hormone therapy was affecting his memory. Clyde would be handling Petunia if she were being cremated. The fact that Eddy and Annette were handling her body as they were instructed clearly meant she was being buried as planned. "I don't understand what the problem is."

"You shouldn't have gone for a walk at such a crucial time." He threw up his hands. "Clyde and Beatrice aren't in today, and Eli is getting the hearse detailed. Gertrude has her hands full at the front desk, manning the phones. I'm not so sure you can handle taking over the business. Thank the lord for Hank." He felt his pulse and started deep breathing.

I rubbed the back of my aching neck as the tension of everything I was juggling weighed me down once more. "Dad, calm down. I'm sure everything will be fine if you tell me what happened."

Collin walked out of his apartment at that moment and looked at us in surprise. "Mortimer. Morti." He nodded his head once in greeting. "I just stepped out to take a break from my writing. How's it going?" He zipped up his black leather jacket against the chill.

Hank walked out of the funeral home, wearing jeans,

work boots, and a flannel shirt with the sleeves rolled up. He pulled his ballcap down lower on his head, then smoothed a hand over his beard as he nodded once to me and then turned to my father. "There doesn't seem to be any major damage down there. I'm just glad I got there in time to let them out."

"Let who out?" I looked at Hank for clarity, since my father was talking in circles and clearly no help. "What is going on?"

"Someone started a fire in the morgue and blocked the doors. Eddy and Annette were stuck down there, but I put the fire out and freed them." He touched my arm. "Everything is going to be okay, Morti. I'll see to it personally."

"I don't think we've officially met," Collin said, stepping forward and holding out his hand. "I'm Collin Quinn."

"Hank Booker." He briefly shook Collin's hand, his gaze still focused on me. "You know where to find me if you need me, Morti."

"Thank you, Hank. I don't know what I would do without you." I rubbed my arms, still in shock over what had happened. A fire in the morgue? We'd never had anything like this happen in all my forty years. Truth sure was stranger than fiction.

Hank tipped his hat to me and went back to work.

"Dad, why didn't Collin's smoke alarm go off upstairs? And what about our sprinkler system?"

"I don't know what's going on, but you can bet I'm going to find out. I'm calling Officer Pickles and Fire Chief

Monroe. If there's something to be found, Don and Wendy will find it." He headed back inside the funeral home, leaving Collin and me alone.

"So, that's the handyman?" Collin stared after Hank with oddly curious narrowed eyes, as he disappeared around back. "I saw him before, but I never actually met him."

I sighed, shifting my weight from one foot to the other. "Yes, that's Hank. He's … helpful." I couldn't quite muster a description that captured the essence of Hank without sounding overly enthusiastic or completely devoid of warmth.

Collin raised an eyebrow, his eyes shimmering with that something I couldn't quite identify that drove me crazy. "How convenient. He's always around when you need him. Sounds like the hero you didn't know you needed." His voice sounded just shy of sarcastic.

"He is pretty handy," I admitted. "But yes, he certainly has a knack for being in the right place at the right time, thank God." I thought about what could have happened if he *hadn't* been around and shivered, crossing my arms over my middle.

Collin lingered for a moment, watching me with those inquisitive eyes that seemed to pierce through my defensive layers. "You okay? You look a bit … rattled. I mean, of course you're rattled after coming back from a walk to this morning's crisis, but did something else happen before that?"

I scoffed, perhaps too defensively, not wanting to get

into my confrontation with Sybil. "I'm perfectly fine. Just dealing with the stress of running a funeral home, planning a bachelor party, and catching a stalker. You know, normal stuff." I waved my hand dismissively as if to shoo away the concern radiating from him.

"Right, because fire is just another day at the office," he replied dryly, and then he frowned. "Wait a minute … wasn't there a fire in the *Veil of Secrets*?"

My eyes widened. "Oh, my God, you're right. In the book, Gideon's girlfriend's house was set on fire just before she was kidnapped."

"And weren't you supposed to be working this morning?" A muscle in Collin's jaw flexed.

I nodded slowly. "I started Petunia's makeup before Eddy and Annette showed up, because I couldn't sleep. Then I left and went for a walk. Do you think the stalker thought it was me down there?"

Maybe running into Sybil wasn't a coincidence after all.

"I don't know, but I don't like it." His stormy gaze bore into mine, holding me captive. "I hope you know Hank isn't the only one who has your back."

When you're not with Sybil, I thought, but simply said, "Thank you, Collin. I appreciate that, but I'm tired of playing the victim. I think it's time I become the hero of my own story." Setting fire to my safe space was crossing the line.

I had to start thinking like Oliver King, and find a way to take this protagonist down.

Chapter Fourteen

It was late October. The entire town had shown up for the celebration of life party for Petunia Pepperdine at the Community Center. Father O'Dority and Sister Mary Agnes had conducted calling hours and a moving funeral for the family, followed by a burial at the best plot in Mayflower's cemetery, with a headstone that outshone all others. Now the celebration of life was for the community.

The Community Center was packed with colorful banners and streamers, draped from the ceiling and walls, with over a century's worth of pictures of Petunia. The tables were covered in festive tablecloths, adorned with centerpieces of fresh flowers and flickering candles.

The scent of freshly cooked food filled the air, mingling with the familiar smells of coffee and tea. The Community Center had taken on the aroma of a warm, welcoming kitchen. The delicious spread of food and drinks offered a variety of flavors and textures, from savory to sweet, and everything in between. The warm, home-made dishes were a reminder of the close-knit community.

The room was buzzing with lively chatter and laughter, as people shared memories and caught up with old friends. The Bedazzled Boomers sat together at one table. Gerty and Gabby Rogers sat with old man Truman Winters, Mayor Edwards and his wife Eleanor, and Principal Brimstone and his wife Bitsy. Zoe and Chaz sat with their children and both of their parents, while Tiffany and Matt sat with their twins, her family, and his stateside relatives. Harmony and Byron sat with her parents and all seven of her brothers, occupying several tables.

Which meant I would sit with my father and Samantha. Her family was gone, but Officer Pickles and Chief Monroe sat with us. Collin walked in alone, looked around, spotted me, and then joined us at our table.

I scanned the room and then looked back at Collin with raised eyebrows. "Where's Sybil?" I spoke quietly for his ears only.

"She left," he said, his gaze locking onto mine. "We broke up."

"I'm sorry," I said, watching him closely. He didn't seem upset.

"I'm not." He shrugged. "That was a very long three months for me. She's nothing like the woman I fell for online. *That* woman challenged me. She was smart and funny and definitely knew what Oliver King was all about.

Sybil is an avid reader, but I honestly don't think she has ever read an Oliver King book." He shook his head. "Maybe she wasn't actually the woman I met online. Or maybe I should have left alone the fantasy of what could be. I never should have met her in person." He looked me in the eyes. "Then again, I never would have met you if I hadn't."

"Collin ..." I wanted to come clean, but I didn't know how.

The interest I saw blazing in his eyes gave me hope there could be something more than friendship between us. It felt wrong not telling him I was the online Sybil he had fallen for. I never should have used Sybil's name as my alias, but in my defense, I really hadn't remembered there was a real Sybil, or I would have chosen a different name. But if I told him the truth now, I could lose him before we even got started.

"It's okay, you don't have to say anything." He smiled, but it didn't quite reach his eyes.

"Now that you're both here," Officer Pickles interrupted, "I wanted to fill you in." He pulled out his notebook.

There'd been no leads on who locked Eddy and Annette in the morgue and set the fire, so I was anxious to hear the next steps.

"The fire department ruled the fire suspicious for now, but Wendy is still investigating. I'm pretty sure there's foul play," Officer Pickles continued, leaning forward with a serious expression. "I've got a gut feeling there's more to it, and I intend to find out what really happened."

I swallowed hard, my stomach flipping.

"Intuition is key in our line of work," Chief Monroe chimed in, her voice felt both authoritative and comforting. She glanced around the room filled with laughter and memories, but quickly shifted back to us. "Keep your eyes open. If anything feels off—anything at all—let us know."

"Good advice for life in Mayflower, I'm finding out," Collin said.

"We're digging deeper into the surveillance footage from the funeral home and surrounding areas, trying to piece together a timeline." Don flipped through the pages of his book until he found what he was looking for.

I nodded, my heart racing. The thought of being under scrutiny sent flutters of anxiety through my stomach. "Have you found anything?"

"Not yet, but we're interviewing everyone who had access to the building," he continued, then glanced around the table. "That includes employees at *Smith's Funeral Home* and anyone who might have seen something unusual that day."

"Great," I muttered, my fingers nervously tracing the edge of my water glass. "I can just see the headlines now: 'Local Mortician Can't Handle the Heat … Literally.'"

Officer Pickles chuckled lightly, but quickly sobered. "This isn't a joke, Morti. You're at the center of it, and we need to treat this seriously." His gaze held mine, heavy with concern.

"Seriously ... like a funeral?" I laughed, desperately trying to deflect the gravity of the situation.

"Exactly. Maybe *yours,* if you're not careful," Chief Monroe interjected, with an eyebrow raised. "You're playing a leading role here, whether you like it or not."

Collin's expression shifted from amusement to genuine worry. "You're not in this alone, Morti. We'll figure this out together." He leaned in closer, and for a moment, everything around us faded into a blur. It was just his intense gaze that anchored me in this whirlwind of uncertainty.

"Together," I echoed, feeling the weight of that word— a promise and a tether. But what if my past mistakes, my little web of deceit, unraveled everything before we even had a chance to stitch new beginnings?

"Morti?" Collin's voice sliced through my thoughts. "You're zoning out on me again. What's going on in that head of yours?"

I glanced at the table—my father animatedly recounting a story to Officer Pickles and Chief Monroe about Petunia's legendary escapades, Samantha nodding along, her expression encouraging. It felt surreal, the atmosphere thick with joy while I was suffocating in dread. "Just thinking about how this feels like one of those moments where you have to decide between flight or fight."

Collin furrowed his brow. "Are you saying you want to run away from this?"

"No." My response came out sharper than intended. "I mean ... yes? But not in the way you think."

"What I think is that we need to investigate," he replied, that spark of mischief returning to his voice. "Let's put on our detective hats, channel our inner Oliver Kings, and dive into this mystery. You said you wanted to become the hero of your own story, right? So, let's not just wait for answers to come to us."

I raised an eyebrow at him, half-excited by the prospect, but half-terrified. "You do realize this isn't some fictional plot twist where we magically uncover the truth in a couple of days, right? This is real life, and it tends to be a lot messier—especially in Mayflower."

"I thrive on messy." The warmth of his presence wrapped around me like a comforting blanket. "It's like a thriller novel waiting to unfold," he murmured, his voice low enough that only I could hear.

"More like a horror story," I replied, eyeing the colorful banners strung above our heads. They felt more like a cruel mockery as they flapped lightly in the air, taunting the impending doom that lurked just outside these walls. A life celebration for someone who had lived vibrantly should have been a happy occasion, yet I couldn't shake the chill crawling up my spine.

Our stalker could be any one of these people, and we wouldn't have a clue.

Suddenly, my father's jovial laughter pierced through my thoughts, drawing my attention back to our table. He appeared blissfully unaware of the storm brewing beneath our surface. Samantha leaned in closer to him, her laughter too bright for this somber gathering. Something twisted in my gut—jealousy or protectiveness, I couldn't tell anymore.

Collin was right. I needed a distraction, and I was through with waiting around for someone else to fix everything.

I looked him in the eyes, took a deep breath, and said, "I'm in."

EVEN WITH OUR renewed fervor for solving our very own personal Oliver King novel, Collin and I still hadn't had any luck in figuring out who might be stalking us. Things had quieted down since the fire, and I didn't get the sense someone was watching me anymore, so I was praying whoever it was had left town.

With Sybil gone from Liberty, Collin and I had been spending a lot of time together. He was still working on his article, and I was still planning my father's bachelor party. Life was good at the moment.

I let myself into Zoe and Chaz's house for our weekly girls' night. Chaz took their children to the movies, and Byron was hanging out with Matt to help with the twins at Matt's house, leaving Tiffany, Harmony, and me alone with Zoe.

The smells of Zoe's French cuisine in her state-of-the-art kitchen were divine.

"Ah, the sweet scent of culinary distraction," I said, taking a moment to inhale deeply. "What are we cooking tonight? Or, should I say, what are *you* cooking while I stand here and drool?"

Zoe chuckled, stirring a bubbling pot on the stove. "Just a little *coq au vin*, hon. But I need all of your hands on deck for dessert. It's my secret family recipe—chocolate lava cake that could make even the most stoic person weep."

"I don't think anyone can withstand the allure of molten chocolate, doll," Tiffany chimed in, her eyes gleaming with excitement as she leaned against the kitchen island. "As long as it's not more of that 'surprise' cake Harmony made last week. Or should I say *tried* to make."

Harmony snorted, her red spiked hair not moving an inch as she laughed. "They were cookies not cake, babe, and definitely not Chocolate Delight like they were supposed to be." She rolled her eyes. "More like 'Chocolate Disaster,' and I'm never attempting to cook for Byron again."

"I'm pretty sure he doesn't care if you can cook or not." I chuckled, inhaling deeply, letting the rich aroma of garlic and fresh herbs wash over me like a warm wave.

The kitchen was a delicate balance of chaos and creativity, with pots bubbling on the stove and a cascade of colorful vegetables arranged haphazardly across the counter. Zoe was a culinary sorceress, conjuring up dishes that tasted as though they were crafted in some Michelin-starred kitchen.

"Thanks, girls. I'm just glad you all could make it," she called from the stovetop, her hands flourished above her head as if presenting an exquisite masterpiece. "Tonight, we're once again embracing our inner Frenchie. You know what that means—wine, cheese, and enough calories to feed a small village."

"Just what I needed after this week." I grinned, hopping onto a barstool and eyeing the decadent spread she had laid out. "I could drown my worries in cheese fondue and diet cola, of course."

"So, spill the tea, babe," Harmony said from the sofa. "I heard Sybil left town."

I sighed, feeling the weight of her question settle on my shoulders like a heavy cloak. "She did," I admitted, picking at the edge of my napkin. "Collin and I are ... well, we're just friends now." I could hear the knowing chuckles from Tiffany and Harmony.

"Just friends?" Tiffany echoed, arching an eyebrow with that infuriating twinkle in her eye. "Please, doll. You two practically glow in the dark together. It's an atomic romance waiting to happen."

I rolled my eyes, but a smile crept onto my lips despite myself. "It's complicated. There was a lot of ... drama with Sybil. And honestly? It's just nice to be normal for once, without all the theatrics of their relationship."

"Normal? Babe, we're baking a dessert that erupts like a volcano," Harmony chimed in, dropping back onto the couch with a dramatic flourish.

"We'll see what happens. I'm afraid once he finds out I was the Cyber Sybil he met online and not the Real Sybil he met in person here in Mayflower, he might never want to speak to me again. I'm not ready for that possibility yet, and I can't start a romantic relationship with him until I tell him the truth. So for now, we're focusing on his article and my father's bachelor party."

"That's understandable," Zoe said, dishing up food for us all and refilling our drinks. "How's the investigation going on the fire in your morgue? Do you really think it could be the person who was stalking you and Collin?"

"Most likely, but it's odd. Ever since the police and fire chief got involved, the stalker has backed off. We haven't had any more incidents or feelings of being watched."

"Well, that's good," Tiffany said. "I was really worried for you."

"You and me both, dude." Harmony shook her head. "That's messed up."

"Tell me about it," I replied, swirling the remnants of my soda in the glass and eyeing the dark liquid as if it might offer me answers. "I mean, it's all a bit too quiet, don't you think? It feels wrong to breathe easy when the air still smells like smoke and secrets."

Zoe placed a steaming bowl of *coq au vin* in front of me, the rich aroma mingling with the sweetness of the impending chocolate delight. "You'll drive yourself crazy worrying about things you can't control, Morti. Focus on what's right in front of you." She nudged me gently with her elbow. "Tonight, let's just enjoy this meal. No mysteries, no stalkers, just drinks and food."

"You're right. I don't want to think about any of that tonight," I said, forcing a smile as I ate a spoonful of food. "Tonight is all about indulgence and good company." But even as I said it, my mind flickered back to the lurking shadows. A sudden chill ran down my spine—a reminder that the past didn't simply fade away.

Tiffany, ever perceptive, must have sensed my wavering spirit. She leaned against the countertop, her expression softening. "Hey, doll, if anything's bothering you, we're here for you. This isn't just about chocolate lava cake—it's about friendship."

I nodded, grateful for their support. "I know. I'm just … trying to figure out how to handle everything without losing myself. The stalker, my dad's wedding plans, and what to do about Collin."

"Morti, listen, babe," Harmony chimed in, her voice steadier than I felt. "You're not the only one with questions about life. None of us have it all figured out. Just take it one day at a time—kind of like how we're tackling this lava cake. One layer at a time."

"Layer? More like a molten mess waiting to happen, with us helping," I laughed, though the laughter felt brittle against the backdrop of my swirling thoughts.

Zoe clapped her hands, the sound breaking through my cluttered mind. "Dessert first, drama second. We'll focus on chocolatey goodness and deal with all our crises later."

The kitchen pulsed with energy as Zoe began mixing together sugar and eggs, the whisk whirring like a tiny cyclone of culinary ambition. I took a moment to appreciate her infectious enthusiasm—her spirit was a buoy that kept us afloat against the tide of uncertainty.

"Okay, let's do this," I declared, channeling my inner baker, then realizing I did that a lot. Put off my problems instead of facing them head on. Sybil was gone, yet I still hadn't talked to Collin.

I began to wonder if I ever would.

Chapter Fifteen

I t was early November, and the day had finally arrived: my father's bachelor and Samantha's bachelorette party. Of course, Sybil had gotten the upper hand one final time before she left. She'd convinced Samantha to have a coed party with my father, knowing full well that wasn't what I wanted. I'd gone along with the idea for my father's sake, because I'd promised him that I would try harder to get along with my future Mommy Dearest.

If it killed me in the process, at least I lived above a funeral home.

The parties took place at *McGinny's Pub,* with all the guests—spanning a few decades—mingling and having a blast. Samantha, her mother, her sister, and several women she'd gotten to know, including Zoe, Tiffany, and Harmony, were in attendance. My father, Tiffany's father, Harmony's father, and several men he'd known forever, including Chaz, Byron, Matt, and his uncle and cousins, were in attendance as well.

All our staff from the funeral home were there, including the newest addition, Hank. Collin was there as well, since he and my father had bonded from the moment he'd rented his apartment. Collin and I were just friends, but with Sybil out of the picture, the chemistry between us had grown, no matter how hard I tried to tamp it down.

The atmosphere of *McGinny's* comforted me like an old, familiar friend, albeit one that smelled faintly of stale beer and the remnants of bad karaoke. The laughter and clinking glasses danced around me, punctuating the thick air with a sense of camaraderie I both craved and feared. I glanced around, searching for a hint of normalcy in this bizarre mix of family dinner and frat party.

"Morti! Over here!" Harmony hollered through the din, waving her arms as if she were trying to signal an airplane. I forced a smile and navigated past groups of revelers, my own discomfort hanging onto my every step like unwanted ankle weights, threatening to drag me down.

Halfway to their table, I caught sight of Collin leaning against the bar, strikingly at ease. He wore a deep-navy shirt that hugged his frame just enough to make me forget myself for a moment. My father was in animated conversation with old man Truman Winters and Mayor Edwards, Samantha laughing a little too heartily at one of his jokes as she stood beside his wife, Eleanor.

Collin's stormy gray eyes caught mine.

For a moment, time seemed to freeze. The noise that

usually filled my mind quieted down; all that existed was the charged atmosphere between us. I felt my heart dance —a bizarre tango of excitement and nerves.

Just friends or not, this was one precarious balancing act.

"Hey! Morti!" Zoe called from across the packed room, motioning me to come like a puppy in training. "Hurry up. Come join us!"

Glancing back at Collin, my heart felt a pang of longing. He was laughing with my father, an expression of genuine mirth lighting up his expressive eyes, and for a moment, I forgot about everything else—the stalker, my tangled emotions, and my family problems.

"Morti! Are you just going to stand there, or are you going to join us before next year?" Tiffany's voice cut through my reverie as she pointed to the empty seat beside her from the group gathered around a table decorated with colorful streamers and over-the-top party hats.

Taking a deep breath, I forced myself to step forward. "I'm coming!" I called back, plastering on a smile. I hated crowds. Tiffany, Tabatha, Zoe, and Harmony were joined by Matt, Finn, Chaz, Byron, and ... Hank. I took the last seat at the table, trying to ignore Collin's burning gaze from across the room.

"Great party, Morticia," Hank's voice was warm and comforting as he spoke softly from the seat beside me.

"Thanks," I replied, forcing down the slight flush that crept up my cheeks. "It's ... something." I gestured vaguely at the raucous celebration, the noise enveloping us like a thick fog. Merging parties had meant co-planning, which had added even more stress for me. I felt suffocated and fought the urge to escape. "I just hope it doesn't turn into a circus act before the night's over."

Hank chuckled, his laughter a soothing balm against my frayed nerves. "With this lot? I'd bet my last dollar it will. Just wait until someone gets ahold of the karaoke machine." His eyes gleamed with mischief as he leaned closer. "But for now, let's enjoy the party. What's your poison?"

"Diet cola. I don't drink."

"Coming right up." He shrugged, then turned to the group. "Anyone need another round?"

Everyone gave their order, and he flagged down a waiter.

"Thanks, Hank," I replied, shifting in my chair as anxiety prickled at the nape of my neck. The din of voices hummed around us, and I focused on centering myself.

"So, what's your plan tonight?" Hank leaned closer, his curiosity genuine. "You gonna show us your secret dance moves, or keep it low-key?"

I chuckled nervously. "I'm sure by now you've gotten to know me—low-key is my middle name. I'm pretty sure it was written on my birth certificate between 'Morticia' and 'Smith.'"

Hank laughed, which eased some of the tension in my chest. "Then we'll have to change that. You've got to embrace the crazy once in a while." He gestured dramatically to the rest of the table, where Chaz had just pulled out an inflatable guitar for an impromptu karaoke session.

"Embrace the crazy? You've clearly never met my family."

His gaze softened. "Okay, no crazy." His eyes met mine with a look I couldn't quite identify. "Care for a dance?"

Before I had a chance to tell him I couldn't dance, he stood and held out his hand. Gazes started turning our way. The one thing I hated more than embarrassing myself was being the center of attention. I quickly slipped my hand into his and let him lead me to the dance floor filled with people so we could blend in.

The dance floor was a whirl of flailing limbs and slightly off-beat rhythms. I felt like a deer caught in headlights as we stepped into the fray, Hank's hand warm around mine—an anchor to something solid amidst the swirling madness. The music thumped like a heartbeat, filling my veins with an energy I hadn't anticipated.

"Just follow my lead," Hank said, his voice low enough to be heard over the noise. He moved effortlessly, guiding me with a confidence that made me feel less like an awkward wallflower and more like a reluctant participant.

I tried to match his rhythm, uncertain if I was succeeding or just flailing in some embarrassing choreography of steps. "This is *so* not my scene," I admitted, laughing nervously as I stumbled over my own feet.

His eyes sparkled with mischief as he spun me around. "That's exactly why you need to let loose. Step out of your comfort zone and take a chance on something new."

Clearly, he didn't know me very well at all.

I could feel a spotlight beam down on me despite the lack of actual illumination. The voices faded into a dull roar, and all I could hear was my heartbeat hammering in my ears like a percussion section gone rogue. Hank's hand was warm around mine, and I found myself wishing for the ability to blend into the background like a shadow.

The music changed to a slow song, and I turned to leave.

He pulled me in tight. "I've got you," he said, his voice low and comforting, cutting through my rising panic.

He began to sway gently, guiding me with a grace that felt so foreign to my rigid demeanor. I mirrored his movements awkwardly, trying not to think about how utterly ridiculous I looked or how every eye in the room was likely glued to us.

"I told you I can't dance," I blurted out, half-laughing as he spun me around, and I nearly stumbled into a nearby table.

"Trust me, Morti—no one's judging you except for maybe that Collin guy over there, staring daggers at us."

I glanced at Collin and quickly looked away, feeling my face flame three shades of red.

"Is he your boyfriend?" Hank studied me closely.

"No, we're just friends."

"Someone might want to tell him that."

"Do you always make women sweat this much on the dance floor?" I joked, changing the subject and trying to mask my nerves with sarcasm as I stumbled slightly over my own feet again.

"Only the special ones," he replied, staring at me so intensely it unnerved me.

"Yes, special friends." I stepped back from him. "Well, I'm exhausted. Thank you for the dance. I should check on my father, since I am the host, after all. See you at work tomorrow."

I walked away before he could say anything more.

Collin intercepted me before I reached my father. "I thought you didn't dance?"

The memory of when we almost danced at Tiffany's wedding reception at this very pub before Sybil pulled him away flashed through my mind's eye. Now he knew how I had felt.

"I don't." I shrugged, raising my chin a notch. "But that doesn't mean I'm opposed to trying with the right partner."

"And Handyman Hank is the right partner?" Collin's jaw hardened.

"Well, he is the only one who asked. So, yes. He's a good friend."

Collin's shoulders relaxed some. "Lucky guy."

"Is he?" I stared at Collin with so many unspoken words left unsaid.

"Morticia, darling," Samantha half squealed. "This is exactly what I wanted."

"I'm glad I made you happy." I looked at my father, who looked more tired than ever. "And how about you, Dad? Are you having fun?"

"Of course, he is, right, Pooh Bear?" Samantha clung to his arm.

He smiled at her with genuine love in his eyes that gave me pause. "I am happy when you're happy, dear."

I frowned. He obviously loved her, and she genuinely seemed to be besotted by him. Who was I to judge? Maybe it was time I gave her an actual chance. I smiled my Mona Lisa smile at them both and said with sincerity, "I glad, and I am really happy for you both."

Samantha blinked back tears. "Thank you, Morti. That means more than you know."

"Thank you, MeMe," my father whispered the nickname he hadn't used since I was little as he pulled me in for a rare hug. He wasn't much for public displays of affection, or at least he never used to be, pre-Samantha.

I blinked back tears of my own. Maybe change wasn't so bad after all.

A WEEK later I was startled awake by an early nor'easter. I peeked out my window to see several inches of snow on the ground. The wind was whipping, and snow was flying, causing whiteout conditions.

Glancing at the clock, it was early morning. Too early for anyone to be at work yet. Grabbing my phone, I sent out a group text telling everyone to stay home. We were closed for today.

Wide awake, I decided I wouldn't be able to sleep, so I

got dressed in yoga pants, fuzzy socks, and a fleece sweatshirt. Suddenly, I was hit with a bout of horrible cramps. Rushing to the bathroom, my fears were confirmed.

I got my period.

My throat clogged, and the tears began to fall. I wasn't pregnant ... again. Apparently, the third time was not the charm. I had to face the reality that even with fertility treatments and insemination at my doctor's office, it wasn't enough.

I couldn't have a baby of my own.

I'd bought top quality sperm, so it had to be that my eggs were no good. It wasn't like I was getting pregnant and then miscarrying. I wasn't getting pregnant at all. There was always adoption, and maybe down the road I might consider it, but right now I just wanted to curl into a ball and lick my wounds. I couldn't keep spending this kind of money and putting myself through heartache month after month.

I was done.

I went to the kitchen to make myself a hot white chocolate. I heated the kettle and added the ingredients to my mug, swirling in the perfect amount of raspberry syrup because I needed a little something extra at the moment. Lifting the mug to take my first sip, a loud bang hit my window. I screamed and dropped my favorite oversized Oliver King mug, shattering the pieces of ceramic everywhere, as I fell on the floor along with it. That was the last straw. I started sobbing uncontrollably.

Stupid hormones.

A knock sounded on my door, but I ignored it, sitting on the floor crying over the mess my life had become. I heard another loud bang, only this time it was Collin, breaking my lock and barging into my apartment.

"What the hell?" he exclaimed, eyes wide as he surveyed the scene. "Morti, are you okay?"

I swiped at my face, trying to wipe away the tears that seemed to flow more freely than the snow raging outside. "Just peachy," I croaked, gesturing to the broken pieces of my beloved mug like it was the symbol of all my failures. "As you can see, I'm living my best life."

Collin knelt beside me, careful to avoid the shards as he picked up a particularly large fragment. "This is a crime scene," he said, with a half-smile that barely reached his concerned eyes. "But let's focus on you for a second. What's going on?"

"Nothing that requires an audience," I sniffed, hugging my knees to my chest like I could somehow shield myself from all things prickly and uncomfortable.

"Morticia Marigold Smith," he said slowly, forcing me to meet his gaze. "When are you going to let someone in? You don't have to do everything alone. You have people who care about you, whether you believe it or not. And I'm one of them."

His sincerity pierced through my despair like a beam of sunlight breaking through storm clouds. "I can't—" I stammered, the words catching in my throat as fresh tears threatened to spill over. "I can't keep putting myself through this. The treatments, the money, and now ... this."

I gestured helplessly to the wreckage of my mug and my dreams. "My hormones are all over the place. I'm a literal mess."

Collin sighed and sat down fully on the floor beside me, his back against the fridge. He crossed his arms over his knees, looking out into the kitchen as if he could see past the mess into some semblance of order. "What if I told you that life doesn't always happen according to your plans? That sometimes you need to pivot?"

"Pivot?" I echoed incredulously, half-laughing through my tears. "How?"

"I know we're just friends, but we can be more than that. You can talk to me."

I let out a shaky breath as his words settled over me, even if the moment felt unreal. Collin was here, in my messy little world, standing amidst the broken pieces of what once made me happy. If I were honest with myself, I felt both grateful and terrified at letting someone in, but maybe it was time.

"It's everything," I finally admitted, my voice barely above a whisper. "My life feels like a series of failures stacked on top of one another—like Jenga, but with my dreams. I can't ..." My voice cracked, and I swallowed hard. "I can't have kids, Collin. And it hurts."

He leaned closer, his all-seeing eyes searching mine for understanding. "I'm sorry," he said softly, brushing a stray hair behind my ear. "You've been through so much already."

"I had hopes—stupid hopes—that this month would be different. And it's not. It's never different."

Collin reached out and pulled me onto his lap, tucking my head beneath his chin, just holding me while my tears fell. The warmth of his body surrounded me like a cocoon, and for a fleeting moment, the world outside faded away. I wished I could nestle deeper into him and forget everything that hurt, but reality was a stubborn beast that dragged me back to my doubts and fears.

"I won't do this again," I mumbled against his chest, feeling the rhythm of his heartbeat beneath my cheek—a steady reminder that life persisted even when mine felt paused. "I can't keep hoping, only to be disappointed."

Collin's arms tightened around me, as if he could absorb my anguish and transform it into something lighter. "Hope is not stupid," he countered gently. "It's brave. It means you care enough to dream."

"But what if I run out of dreams?" I challenged, my voice muffled by the fabric of his shirt. "What if I've already used them all up?"

"Morti," he murmured, his voice a low rumble, almost reverent. "You're not defined by what you can't do. You're so much more than that."

I closed my eyes, wishing I could believe him, but the doubt lingered. "What if I am? What if that's all I ever will be?"

"You're allowed to feel this way," he murmured into my hair, and I closed my eyes, letting the waves of emotion crash against me, causing me to feel things I hadn't felt in years ... if ever. "You don't have to apologize for it."

I sighed deeply, allowing myself to sink into the vulnerability of the moment. "What if I'm just not meant to be a mother?" The words slipped out, heavy like lead.

"Then you find another way to share your love," he replied gently, rubbing circles on my back.

I snuggled in deeper, letting his words sink in. Could we really be more than just friends? Could he care about me enough that he would forgive my lie? Could I take a chance and share my love with him?

As if reading my thoughts, he slowly lifted my face until I was looking up at him. His gaze searched mine, and then, as if in slow motion, he lowered his head until his lips touched mine. Soft and tender at first and then he parted my lips with his own and slipped his tongue inside.

Pure raw electricity surged between us.

He tasted of coffee and spice and something uniquely him. His arms tightened around me, and I slid mine up around his neck. I couldn't get enough of him. His taste, his smell, his body. He kept running his hands over me as if he felt the same and then laid me down onto my back. Running his hand down my fleece sweatshirt, he slid his palm beneath the bottom and caressed my bare flesh, working his way up toward my aching breast.

"Morti, where are you?" My father hollered from the hallway.

Collin smoothly rolled off me and helped me to my

feet all in one motion, which was a good thing since my legs were Jello.

"Are you okay?" He rushed in through the open, broken door, out of breath and clearly concerned.

"She fell on some spilled cocoa and broke her mug, but I inspected her." He cleared his throat. "She's okay."

"Are you sure? Her face looks awfully flushed, and her eyes are swollen."

"I'm fine, Dad, really," I managed to get out. "It hurt when I fell, but it's all good now. Collin came to my rescue and made everything better." My eyes met his, saying everything I couldn't.

"Well, thank the Lord for Collin. I came to check on you as soon as I heard the storm. You closed the funeral home, and it's a good thing. There's a tree down, blocking the driveway. I had to park on the road and trudge through the snow to get to you." He took off his coat and sat at the table. "Got anymore coffee? I thought we could go over wedding plans, since you have the day off, and I'm here. Or did you and Collin have research plans?" He looked between the two of us curiously.

"Nope. All set, sir. I have an article to finish."

"Then we won't keep you," my father said. "I'll get Hank to fix the door later when the snow lets up."

"Ah, right." Collin set his jaw, leveling me with a look I couldn't decipher. "That handyman sure is handy."

"That he is." My father beamed. "Don't you agree, Morti?"

I nodded, not knowing what to say.

"I'll let myself out." Collin waved at my father and nodded once to me.

"You know where I am if you need any more help with that article," I hollered after him.

"That I do," he said, and left without another word.

Chapter Sixteen

The following week, we all met at *Lolita's Place* for Samantha's wedding shower. Her mother, Wilma, and sister, Lila, rented the back room. There were games and even a raffle: bring a negligee and be entered to win the gift basket full of wine, wine glasses, chocolate, cheese, and crackers.

I was really trying to be nicer and more accepting of Samantha, but I drew the line at buying her lingerie to sleep with my father. Thank God my girls were invited so I didn't have to attend this party alone. We sat at a table together, watching Samantha open her gifts.

I glanced around the room. Samantha and I were the complete opposite. The pastel decorations and frilly table-cloths seemed to smother me. If you could drown in ruffles, I'd be six feet under by now.

Wincing as Samantha unwrapped yet another mono-grammed towel set, Harmony leaned over to me with a disinterested look plastered on her face. "You'd think she was getting a lifetime supply of toilet paper," she whispered. "Now that would be a useful gift."

"Right?" I shrugged. "Honestly, I'd rather see her open something interesting. Like a book—or maybe a body pillow shaped like a giant doughnut."

"Now you're talking!" Harmony chuckled, earning our table a few disapproving looks.

Samantha pulled out yet another kitchen gadget—this time a lemon zester that looked more complicated than any of my college math finals.

Lila, with her light blonde hair and exaggerated gestures, squealed every time Samantha unveiled another item. A set of matching towels, a decorative cheese board, and a rather extravagant bread-maker made their triumphant debut, each eliciting another round of giggles from the gaggle of women gathered around.

I snuck glances at my friends, who were equally amused and horrified by the whole spectacle.

"Why would you need fancy towels for a kitchen?" I murmured to Zoe, who sat beside me sipping her wine like it was the nectar of the gods.

"It's called being 'domesticated,' Morti," she said quietly, then shot me a teasing wink. "You wouldn't understand if you don't like to entertain guests."

"Or a Pinterest account," Tiffany chimed in with hushed tones. "They have boards for everything. I hear they even have an entire board dedicated to how to make small talk at wedding showers."

I chuckled lightly, grateful for the distraction. The gift opening was almost done, and the raffle would start soon. The last thing I wanted was to take part in that.

"Morti!" Lila called out, her voice a little too bright for my taste. "What about you? Are you Team Naughty or Team Nice? Please tell me you brought something to the raffle?"

Great. All eyes turned toward me.

I glanced over at the pile of brightly wrapped gifts sprawled before Samantha, glimmering with the sheen of forced excitement. "I'm Team Indifferent. Just here for moral support." I forced a smile that felt like it might crack under pressure.

"C'mon, it'll be fun!" Lila insisted, waving me over. "You could even make a statement. We all know Samantha has some questionable taste."

"Hey!" Samantha swatted her sister playfully. "I have great taste. Look who I chose for a partner. Right, Morti?"

"You chose the best," I said, biting back, *'but did he?'*

Be nice, be nice, be nice, I repeated over and over in my mind as Samantha shrieked over yet another pastel kitchen gadget that would likely become a dust collector within the first month of their marriage. I couldn't help but picture my father trying to navigate those gadgets with his thinning gray hair and naïve charm, and the thought twisted in my stomach like a nail. *He's a grown man, Morticia. He'll figure it out.*

"Okay, ladies, it's time for the raffle," Wilma said, all class and sophistication, so unlike her daughters. "Back in my day, a woman chose her wedding trousseau based on class and elegance, not on the least amount of see-through fabric available. What if you give poor Mortimer a heart attack?"

Finally, someone with some common sense.

"Oh, Mother, you're so funny. Age is just a number, and my Pooh Bear is as viral as a stallion." Samantha giggled.

And that's my cue to leave.

I pushed back my chair slowly, standing up to escape the clutches of pastel hell. "Excuse me for just a moment." I made my way toward the restroom, hoping for a few seconds of solitude. As I waddled through the throng of giggling women, I couldn't help but overhear snippets of conversation: "Did you see that last gift? It was so cute!" and "Oh my gosh, Samantha is going to look amazing in that negligee!"

Ugh. The thought of my father seeing anything 'cute' with Samantha in it churned my stomach like a blender set on high speed. The restroom door swung shut behind me, and I took a deep breath, allowing the brief sanctuary devoid of color to wash over me.

I splashed some cold water on my face and stared at my reflection. The girl looking back at me was wearing an expression that seemed more suited for a funeral than a wedding shower. A stark reminder that life continued to move forward whether I wanted it to or not.

I left the bathroom and turned in the opposite direction of the small hallway. Just as I planned to escape through the back exit, I bumped straight into Hank.

"Oof! Morti!" He steadied me, his hands firm on my shoulders. "Where'd you come from? I didn't see you there."

"Sorry, Hank, just a bit overwhelmed by all the ... excitement in there," I said, gesturing vaguely toward the noise of the shower.

"Excitement? Is that what we're calling it?" He laughed softly, an easy grin spreading across his face. "Looks more like a pastel explosion."

"Exactly!" I laughed nervously, relieved to be away from the pastel suffocation, even if just for a moment. "I was thinking of making my escape for my own mental health."

Hank raised an eyebrow. "What's wrong with a little pastel explosion? It adds color to the world, don't you think?" He leaned against the wall, arms crossed over his chest, and that grin of his was infectious.

"Color? More like a pop art representation of my worst nightmares." I leaned back against the wall, feeling the cool wood behind me. "I can't believe my dad is about to marry a woman whose taste runs toward everything that sparkles and squeaks. It's like a circus in there, and he's never been a ringleader."

He chuckled softly, the sound warm and inviting. "You know, Morti, I think you need to let yourself have some fun. Life isn't all funerals and books. Want to step outside for some fresh air?"

"More than anything." I nodded, grateful for his understanding.

The back door to *Lolita's Place* creaked open, and the cold breeze slid past us like a smirking specter. We stepped outside, and I let the sharp air prick my cheeks and clear the fog from my mind. Snowflakes danced around us, but all I could think about were the ruffled horrors waiting for me back inside. Hank leaned against the wall just outside the entrance, arms crossed, exuding an aura of easy steadiness.

"I fixed the lock on your door while you were gone. I hope you don't mine. That Collin guy really did a number on it." He studied me closely.

"Thanks." I shrugged. "He heard me scream and was concerned. That's all."

Hank ignored the last part of my response. "So, how's your literary world treating you?" he asked, tilting his head in curiosity. "You've got quite the collection of books."

I chuckled bitterly. "Just peachy, considering my current reality involves more plot twists than Oliver King can write."

"Yeah, his books aren't really my thing, but if you're looking for a good drama, I have loads of recommendations."

"Oh, I think I've had about as much drama as I can take in one lifetime."

He glanced toward the door with roaring laughter coming from inside. "Something tells me your drama has only just begun."

LATER THAT NIGHT, I donned my flannel pajamas and curled up with a blanket on my couch. I reached for my copy of *Veil of Shadows* to study it for more clues. Even though our stalker was still lying low ever since the fire, I wanted to be prepared in case he or she resurfaced.

I frowned. It wasn't there.

I got up and searched all the spots I kept my books with no luck. While I was up, I made myself a cup of tea and threw the teabag wrapper away. Just as I was about to close the trash lid, I noticed a book stuffed down deep near the broken ceramic pieces of my mug.

My father didn't like that I spent so much time alone with my books. Did he throw this away the night he helped me clean up the mess? He tended to move my things around often even though he knew I hated that. I would have to tell him my books were off limits ... especially my Oliver King books. Or an even scarier thought ... had someone slipped into my apartment before Hank had fixed the lock?

Taking my book and my tea back over to the couch, I opened my laptop and logged onto *The King's Quills*, noticing the gang was all there.

Stacy Rose: *Oh, my goodness, I'm so glad to see you here, Morti. We were so worried when we heard about the fire in your morgue. Collin's been keeping us up-to-date since you've been busy juggling all the things you've had going on.*

Morticia Smith: *Oh, he has, has he?*

My heart skipped a beat. I hadn't been able to stop thinking about that kiss and everything it had stirred up inside me. Obviously, Collin didn't feel the same way. I hadn't seen him since we'd made out. I had been so busy lately, I hadn't been online in a while. It made me mad that he could show up and talk to them but not me.

What had freaked him out by our kiss?

She Wolf: *Yeah, do you really think it could have been started by your stalker? I hope it's not a foreshadowing of the Veil of Secrets where Gideon's girlfriend gets kidnapped.*

Collin Quinn: *No one's getting kidnapped.*

Morticia Smith: *Oh, so you do care.*

Why did I just say that? I squeezed my eyes shut and shook my head. That man infuriated me sometimes.

Collin Quinn: *Of course, I care. We're friends, after all.*

Hans Brewmeister: *Sounds like more than friends to me, and here we go off topic again.*

Tie Dye Dotty: *Not off topic, Hans. Veil of Secrets is an Oliver King book, and this crazy person is playing out the plot in real life.*

Hans Brewmeister: *What's crazy is discussing his first book when we haven't even finished his current book.*

Captain Rogers: *Ahoy, young whippersnapper. Quinn is just trying to protect his girl like Gideon Wolfe did.*

Marky Mouse: *Ah, but Gideon Wolfe failed in that book.*

Morticia Smith: *And I'm not Collin's girl.*

Stacy Rose: *Not yet.*

Morticia Smith: *Not likely.*

He'd made that perfectly clear when he'd ghosted me after kissing me. Had it really been that awful for him? My face burned with embarrassment, and I wanted nothing more than to crawl under my blanket and disappear. The banter continued like a tightrope walk, balancing precariously between humor and the uncomfortable truth I was trying to ignore. And where was Collin? I could see he was still online, yet he sat back, letting me deal with this conversation alone.

She Wolf: *Just admit it, Morti. You like him. It's all so romantic.*

I hesitated, my fingers hovering over the keyboard. A part of me wanted to deny it vehemently, but the other half —the one that felt fluttery and stupid when I thought about Collin—silenced me. The blinking cursor mocked my indecision.

Collin Quinn: *Sorry, folks. Nature called. What'd I miss?*

Marky Mouse: *Your love life being played out for everyone to see.*

Tie Dye Dotty: *It's okay to like someone, Morti. It doesn't mean you have to run away.*

Captain Rogers: *No truer words were ever spoken,*

my love. Now what say ye stop running away from me, Dotty?

Tie Dye Dotty: *Oh, Captain, you're so dramatic. I'm not running ... I'm just not sailing away with you. And we're not talking about us. We're talking about Morti and Collin.*

Collin Quinn: *Okay, okay, let's give the poor woman a break. Nothing like putting her on the spot.*

Hans Brewmeister: *Okay, then, let's put the spotlight on you. Do you like Morti?*

Collin Quinn: *What's not to like?*

I could almost hear his voice in my head, teasing but sincere. He was so confusing. The warmth from my tea faded as I stared at the screen, caught in the web of my own thoughts. Wasn't that what I'd done? Run away from everything? From my father moving on, my mother's drinking then dying, my own identity, giving birth, telling Collin the truth? I was so afraid he would leave me once he found out that it was easier for me to cast the blame on him and leave him first.

Morticia Smith: *On that note, I've gotta run.*

Collin Quinn: *And that's what you call a cliffhanger.*

Chapter Seventeen

A faint knock echoed through the dark and still apartment, shattering the silence of the night. The dim blue light from my laptop screen blinked off as I closed it with a soft click and made my way over to answer the door. My heart raced in anticipation, knowing exactly who was on the other side.

Collin.

I hesitated before unlocking the door, peering through the peephole to confirm his identity. Sure enough, he stood there, his usually immaculate dark hair tousled from running his fingers through it in frustration. I opened the door and leaned against the frame, watching him with a mix of curiosity and caution.

"Hi, neighbor," he said, his voice uncertain as he shifted on his feet.

"Long time no see," I replied, standing up straighter.

"I know, I'm sorry for my absence. Can we talk?"

I hesitated for a moment before stepping back to let him in. As he entered, I caught a strong whiff of whiskey on his breath. He headed towards my living room couch, his steps quick and impatient.

"Do you want something to drink?" I called after him, already making my way to the kitchen.

"Whiskey if you have it. If not, I have some next door," he replied without turning around.

"Just because I don't drink doesn't mean I don't have alcohol in my house for entertaining," I muttered under my breath as I poured him a glass. "On the rocks?" I asked over my shoulder.

"Neat is good," he responded, sinking down onto the plush couch and resting his elbows on his knees.

Making myself a cup of herbal tea, steam wafting up to fill the space between us, I joined him on the couch and tucked my legs beneath me so that I could face him directly. "So ... what do you want to talk about?" I asked, trying to keep any hint of nervousness out of my voice.

"I owe you an apology," Collin began, fiddling with the glass in his hands.

"I'm listening," I said, my eyes fixed on his handsome face.

"I'm sorry for ghosting you," he continued, still avoiding eye contact.

"Can I ask why you did?" I prodded gently.

"I haven't been able to stop thinking about kissing you that night," he admitted, finally meeting my gaze with a mix of regret and longing.

"Then why haven't you talked to me since then?"

He shrugged. "I got jealous."

"Of what?" I pressed, wanting to understand.

"Hank fixing your door instead of me," Collin muttered, looking away again.

"I didn't ask him to, my father did," I explained, feeling a surge of frustration at the memory.

"I know. I just got in my head," Collin sighed, running a hand through his hair in a gesture of frustration.

"Why? Hank is my employee, nothing more."

"Does he know that?" Collin echoed Hank's same thoughts about him with a hint of insecurity in his voice.

"Why does it matter? Until that kiss, you and I haven't been anything but friends, and honestly, I have no clue what we are now?" I replied, feeling a mix of confusion and irritation at the situation.

"I know, and that's my fault. I like you a lot, Morti. I've been drawn to you from the first day that I met you, but I owed it to myself and to Sybil to see if there was anything more to our online relationship in person. It turns out, there wasn't. She was nothing like the woman I fell for," he said, his deep voice laced with regret and vulnerability.

"She wasn't?" My heart skipped a beat at his words.

He looked at me intently. "You are more like the Sybil I fell for than she is. And then Handyman Hank had to show up, and all my old fears resurfaced. My ex-wife cheated on me behind my back with my best man. She wasn't the person I thought she was, and it damn near killed me. I can't take that kind of deception again. I thought maybe you and Hank had something going on. I just couldn't take falling for you and then having you leave me for another man, too."

"So you removed yourself from the situation by ignoring me," I concluded, understanding dawning on me … understanding and guilt, as I saw the pain in his eyes caused by a past betrayal.

Collin's expression was remorseful as he nodded, the sorrow clear in his eyes. "It was safer than having my heart broken," he explained, "but seeing you online tonight made me realize how much I miss you. I don't want to keep running anymore."

I felt a twinge of empathy for him, knowing all too well the feeling of constantly fleeing from one's troubles.

"Can I ask why you don't drink?" Collin inquired after a moment of silence, his voice filled with genuine curiosity.

I hesitated before answering, deciding to open up and share my vulnerability just as he had. "My mother was an alcoholic. It nearly destroyed their marriage," I began, my voice softening as I delved into the painful stories my father had told me. "But when she got pregnant with me, she stopped drinking. My father finally saw hope of getting the love of his life back, but then she died during childbirth, and he hasn't been the same since. At least, not the man he tells me he used to be."

"Do you fear becoming like her if you drink?" Collin asked gently.

The question struck deep within me, and I found myself confessing, "As silly as it sounds, yes. I could never do that to my father again, or to myself. That's why I was terrified to give birth as well, but that's no longer an issue."

"I understand," he said quietly, reaching out to lightly touch my hand in a comforting gesture. "He seems happy now with Samantha."

A pang of sadness hit me as I admitted, "I hate to say it, but you're right. I'm not good with change and it's always just been the two of us. I feel like I'm losing him."

"I don't think that's possible," Collin reassured me with a small smile, causing a flutter in my chest.

Despite his reassurance, a heavy sigh escaped my lips as I spoke up again. "But he doesn't need me anymore." My voice was filled with a mixture of sadness and longing.

"Maybe that's not such a bad thing," Collin replied, his thumb gently caressing the back of my hand.

Looking up at him through watery eyes, I couldn't help but confess, "You're right, but I don't want to be alone." Taking a deep breath, I tried to hold back the tears threatening to spill over. "That's why I wanted a baby so badly, to have someone to love. And now I can't even have that."

Collin's expression softened and he spoke softly, "Perhaps not a baby, but you can still have love." His words were filled with understanding and offered a glimmer of hope in the midst of my pain.

As our gazes locked, I could feel the heat radiating off his body, matching my own intense desire. Knowing I had to tell him the truth before things went any further, I began speaking up. "Collin, I—"

But Collin surprised me by interrupting, his voice

thick with longing. "I know, me too." With that, he swooped down and claimed my lips in a possessive kiss.

All rational thoughts fled from my mind as I lost myself in the moment. Wrapping my arms around his neck, I pulled him closer, as our tongues danced together in passionate harmony. The touch of his hands on my skin sent electric sparks shooting through my body, igniting a fire within me that consumed all other thoughts.

Tears streamed down my face, but Collin brushed them away gently without breaking the kiss.

"It's okay, baby," he whispered against my throat as he trailed kisses down to my collarbone while peeling off my shirt and bra. Gazing at me with awe, he admired my naked form with reverence. "You're so damn beautiful."

In that moment, I felt beautiful and desired, completely free of self-consciousness and intimidation.

"Collin, I need you," I pleaded breathlessly.

Without hesitation, he lifted me into his arms and carried me to my bed, laying me down gently as if I were the most precious thing in the world.

My body trembled with anticipation as I tried to sit up, but he pressed me back down with a firm yet gentle hand. His touch sent shivers down my spine as he ran his hands over my breasts, teasing my nipples with light touches that made me crave more.

A low chuckle escaped his lips before he replaced his fingers with his mouth. He expertly flicked my nipple with the tip of his tongue before taking it into his warm mouth and sucking hard. The sensation sent shockwaves through my body, and I arched my back in response, moaning with pleasure. My fingers tangled in his hair as I pulled him closer.

He momentarily pulled away before stripping me of my yoga pants and underwear until I lay fully naked before him. His eyes blazed with desire as he peeled off his own t-shirt and sweatpants, standing before me in all his magnificence.

"You're beautiful," I whispered, reaching out to stroke his erection.

This time, it was his turn to moan before lying down beside me on the bed. I ran my hands over his smooth, muscular body, needing to feel every inch of him. He was real and alive and all mine. I rolled him onto his back, wanting to possess him completely before he slipped away.

As if sensing my urgency, he relaxed against the pillows and reassured me in a soft voice, "I'm not going anywhere, baby."

Our eyes locked as I traced my nails lightly over his chest and pinched his nipples. A muscle in his jaw clenched, but he didn't move. My mouth followed suit, leaving a trail of kisses and licks down his stomach until I reached his impressive erection. I stroked him slowly, reveling in the feel of him in my hand before taking him into my mouth and sucking hard.

A guttural groan escaped Collin's throat, and he flipped me over onto my back. "My turn," he growled before lowering himself between my legs.

He worshipped every inch of my body with his lips

and tongue, sending waves of pleasure coursing through me. It was like nothing I had ever experienced before—being cherished, worshipped ... loved. His hands followed the path of his mouth as he stopped at my bellybutton and dipped his tongue, then fingertip inside, causing me to buck my hips in response.

"Collin, I want—" I managed to gasp out before he parted my folds and began stroking me with his thumb.

My body responded immediately, arching towards him as he dove in with his tongue and sent me spiraling into ecstasy. I screamed his name, gripping the sheets tightly and thrashing my head back and forth on the pillow as he expertly brought me to multiple mind-blowing orgasms.

My body trembled beneath him as he slid inside me, filling me with an intensity I never thought possible. We locked eyes, our bodies still as we took in the gravity of this moment.

It was then that I realized I loved him.

What started as a simple online flirtation had blossomed into something much deeper and more profound over the past five months. I wanted to tell him everything, to pour out my heart and soul, but before I could, he began to move.

With each powerful thrust, he claimed me completely. Our bodies were perfectly attuned to one another, like two pieces of a puzzle finally fitting together. My love for him could wait; right now, I needed him too much. I surged against him, seeking to be closer, and he matched my every movement with equal fervor. With each stroke, the pressure built until it was almost unbearable.

In that moment of pure ecstasy, I screamed his name as my body convulsed in pleasure. He followed soon after, calling out my name as we both collapsed in a heap, our hearts racing and bodies entwined.

Hours passed as we made love again and again, lost in each other's embrace until exhaustion finally claimed us. In the early morning hours, I awoke to a chill that seemed to seep into my bones. My eyes slowly opened, taking in the sight of Collin sitting at the edge of the bed.

His body was tense and naked, his face cast in shadows.

My heart began to race as a sense of unease settled over me. Something was wrong.

Desperately pulling the covers up to my chest, I sat up and tried to speak. But his voice cut through the silence, sharp and cold like an icicle.

"It's a little late for that, don't you think?" His words were filled with accusation and anger, unlike anything I had ever heard from him before.

Panicked and confused, I asked, "What's going on, Collin? I'm confused."

He showed me—my copy of *Behind the Mask*, filled with notes scrawled in the margins with ideas for a rewrite that could have only come from one person ... Cyber Sybil.

"You're her, aren't you?" he said, in a quiet voice filled with hurt and disappointment.

Reaching out for him, I pleaded, "Please, Collin, let me explain. You don't understand."

"So, you're telling me that you're not the Sybil I met online?" He looked at me with desperate eyes.

I couldn't lie anymore. "Well, no, but—"

His face fell. "That's all I need to hear." He turned away, dressing himself quickly while I sat there, feeling exposed and vulnerable. "It's too late for explanations now," he said in barely more than a whisper. "I don't know what kind of game you're playing, but I'm not interested in being duped. I've been there before."

Tears streamed down my face as my worst fear became reality. "I tried to tell you," I sobbed.

"You should have tried harder." His words were like daggers piercing my heart as he looked at me with so much dissolution and hurt. "Or was it fun for you to make a fool out of me?"

Desperate to make him see the truth, I cried out, "That wasn't my intention at all. I love you!"

But it was too late. He looked at me with pain in his eyes before delivering the final blow. "I'm sorry, but I just can't do this anymore."

My heart shattered as he walked out of my life, leaving me alone with my lies and regrets, the weight of his words heavy on my shoulders. I could only watch as he disappeared into the darkness, taking a piece of me with him.

Chapter Eighteen

I had become a recluse, trapped in my apartment for a week without even venturing out to work. My father had grown concerned and reached out to my friends, who were now gathered around me in my living room. Tears streamed down my face as I blew my nose, the last tissue in yet another box crumpled in my hand. My nostrils were raw and tender from constant use, but no amount of discomfort could stop the tidal wave of emotions coursing through me.

Zoe, with her ever-present empathy, placed a new box of tissues in front of me. Her eyes filled with understanding as she said softly, "My heart is breaking for you."

Tiffany wrapped her arms around me in a comforting hug. "I still can't believe he's really gone," she whispered. "But he loved you so much, it was obvious to everyone."

I shook my head, unable to hold back the sobs that wracked my body. "He paid his lease in full and turned over the keys. He's definitely gone," I choked out. "When he found out I was Cyber Sybil, any feelings he may have had for me died instantly. I could see the hurt and disappointment in his eyes."

Harmony, always trying to lift spirits with sugary treats, handed me a bowl of ice cream. But even the thought of indulging couldn't distract me from my grief. "He's just angry, babe," she said soothingly. "Deep down, he still loves you."

"He never said he loved me. He just said he couldn't do this anymore," I muttered, pushing the bowl away. "I don't even know where he is, because he doesn't have a home. He travels from place to place for work. He's gone and he's not coming back."

Zoe reached out and took my hand in hers. "Morti, you can't just sit here and wallow," she urged, her eyes pleading with me to snap out of it. "You have people who care about you, even if Collin isn't one of them anymore."

I looked down at the pile of crumpled tissues in my lap, feeling lost and alone. "It's different for you guys," I mumbled, wiping at my tears. "You haven't invested months of your life into a false identity, only to have it ripped away in an instant."

Tiffany leaned in closer, her brow furrowed with concern. "But this isn't just about him," she said gently. "It's about you finding yourself again after everything that's happened. You've been lost for so long, Morti. We were happy to finally see you coming out of your shell and enjoying life."

A pang of regret twisted in my stomach as I thought about all the times I had tried to fit into someone else's expectations, whether it was as Cyber Sybil or the perfect daughter. I was tired of playing roles and wearing masks.

"You're right," I admitted. "It's time for me to focus on myself and stop trying to be something I'm not."

As the words settled in my mind, the heaviness in my chest began to lift, even if just a little. I could feel the warmth of my friends surrounding me like a protective barrier against the mess that had engulfed my life.

"There's a whole world out there waiting for you, Morti," Zoe encouraged, her eyes brightening with renewed determination. "You've got all this potential just bubbling under the surface. Why not embrace it instead of running away from it?"

A flicker of hope sparked within me. Maybe this was my chance to break free from the self-imposed shackles I had worn for so long. The idea seemed both terrifying and exhilarating.

"Okay," I said hesitantly. "I'm going to do something totally out of my comfort zone, like starting an in-person book club. And I'll hold the first meeting at my place. Maybe I'll even choose a genre other than a thriller. Hank mentioned he could recommend a good drama."

"Count me in. I love to read," Zoe said.

"Dramas are my cup of tea. I'll be there," Tiffany added.

"I'm not much of a reader, but you can count on me just the same." Harmony nodded.

My friends' unwavering support gave me the courage to step outside of my comfort zone and start living life on my own terms again.

My stomach churned with unease at the thought of being surrounded by strangers, but the comforting presence of my friends by my side helped to calm my nerves.

"I'll even whip up some delicious snacks," I declared, feeling a spark of excitement ignite within me. "Maybe a fancy cheese platter or something. It'll be like our girls' nights, but bigger and better. How hard could it be?"

Zoe's face lit up with pride. "Morti, you are going to be an amazing hostess. I can already see it."

"And we'll bring drinks," Tiffany chimed in, her eyes twinkling mischievously. "To give us some liquid courage, of course."

Harmony clapped her hands together in excitement. "This is going to be epic. Just imagine it—a room full of people sipping cocktails and passionately discussing emotional dramas, just in time for the holiday season."

I could already picture it in my mind's eye, like one of those vibrant scenes from my cherished novels. A place where words would connect us beyond our masks and facades. But beneath all the excitement, a nagging doubt lingered, whispering that I was still that awkward girl from the funeral home who always lingered on the edges of parties, like a ghost.

"What if no one shows up?" I anxiously bit my bottom lip.

Zoe put a reassuring hand on my shoulder. "Then we'll

have our own book club girls' night. But remember, I am a professional party planner. If we do this event right, people will show up."

Determined to overcome my fears and doubts, I made a shaky but resolute decision. "Okay, let's do it. You plan the event, and I'll reach out to Hank to pick our first book."

My friends erupted into cheers and rallied around me, their excitement bubbling like fizzy soda. I felt something building inside of me—maybe it was courage, or maybe it was just the hope that this book club could be my salvation from the constant cycle of grief and isolation that had become my norm.

"Let's make it happen," Zoe said, giving me a gentle nudge. "We'll turn your place into a cozy haven with fairy lights and delicious snacks, and we can even dress up for the occasion. Book-themed costumes, anyone?"

Tiffany let out an exaggerated groan. "Oh no, please spare us all. The last thing I need is to show up looking like a character from some stuffy Victorian novel while trying to sip wine without spilling it all over myself."

Harmony joined in on the laughter. "Just imagine Morti as Jane Eyre."

I shuddered at the thought. "Let's not get ahead of ourselves. Baby steps are more my speed."

Zoe hugged me tightly. "Any step forward is progress. You talk to Hank about picking a book, and I'll take care of the rest. This is a good thing, Morti. You've got this."

I took a deep breath and nodded, knowing that taking charge of my life and moving forward was something I desperately needed to do. But despite all the encouragement, I couldn't shake off the sense of impending doom, as if this whole book club idea was one big mistake.

EXHAUSTION AND RELIEF washed over me as I finally allowed myself a moment to breathe. My workload had been suffocating, leaving me with barely enough time to keep up with everything that needed to be done. In fact, it had taken me an entire week just to catch up on everything.

Meanwhile, Zoe had taken it upon herself to plan my book club as promised, and the word spread like wildfire. Her exceptional marketing skills had already garnered interest from several potential members.

Now all that was left for me to do was to choose the first book and give everyone enough time to read it. But before I could fully relax, I called in Hank. He'd been helping my father in my absence. It had been two weeks since I last saw him.

"Hank, can I have a moment of your time?" I motioned for him to come into my office before he left for the day.

He respectfully removed his hat with a nod. "Of course, Ms. Smith. What can I do for you?"

I furrowed my brow at the formal address. "Please, call me Morti. And why so proper all of a sudden?"

He shrugged nonchalantly. "I thought that's what you wanted."

With a sigh of frustration, I admitted, "I haven't been clear with anyone, including myself, about what I want. But I'm working on changing that."

"Is this about the book club?" He raised an eyebrow, his voice tinged with curiosity.

"Yes," I confirmed, a sly Mona Lisa smile playing on my lips. "I need your help."

His face lit up with genuine eagerness. "I'm glad you asked. How can I assist?"

"I need a recommendation for our first book." I could still feel the emptiness inside from Collin's sudden departure, but I forced a brave smile. It was time for something new.

Hank blinked in surprise, his brow furrowing in thought. "A drama? But I thought you and Collin were both into thrillers."

My heart twisted at the mention of Collin's name, but I pushed down the familiar pain. "Collin isn't here anymore, and it's time for something different."

"I wondered why I hadn't seen him around, but I didn't want to pry. I'm not much into gossip." Hank's expression turned serious, his eyes searching mine. "Did he leave?"

I nodded, swallowing the lump in my throat.

"Is he coming back?" His voice sounded tense.

"I don't think so." My voice wavered as I fought back tears.

Hank's gaze locked onto mine, his eyes probing. "I wouldn't be so sure about that. You're a remarkable woman

... but enough about that." He cleared his throat. "About the book ... I have a few options at my place. If you have a moment, we can go over them."

Relieved to have a distraction from my thoughts, I accepted his offer. "I'm all yours."

"I was hoping you'd say that." Hank led the way out to the parking lot, gesturing towards his truck. "We can take my truck. The roads are pretty treacherous right now."

As we drove through town and headed towards the outskirts, large snowflakes began to fall heavily, creating a thick curtain of white that obscured our surroundings.

Frowning, I asked, "Where do you live?" It dawned on me that I had never asked before.

I had just assumed that he was staying at the *Mayflower Inn* until he found a more permanent place to rent or buy. But it had been months since we hired him as our new assistant, and I had been too preoccupied with myself to update our records with his new address. A sudden thought hit me.

That meant no one could find out where we were going.

"I found an old cabin," Hank replied simply, his eyes focused on the road ahead. He turned off the main road and onto a dark dirt path through the woods, and my unease only grew stronger.

"In the woods? Who rents a cabin in the middle of nowhere?" I couldn't help but ask.

Hank didn't answer and instead drove on in silence, his foot heavy on the gas pedal as if in a hurry. When we finally arrived at our destination in complete darkness, my unease turned into genuine fear. The secluded cabin looked like something out of a horror movie, with its peeling paint and broken windows.

He cut off the engine and turned to face me, his eyes no longer warm, but cold and full of malice.

"I changed my mind," Hank sneered, his voice low and menacing. "It turns out I'm in the mood for some thrills after all." A shiver ran down my spine as he reached towards me. "Let's play out the ending of a different book ... *Veil of Secrets.*"

My mind raced as I tried to remember the plot of that book—Detective Gideon Wolfe's girlfriend gets kidnapped in a cabin in the woods ...

"You're the stalker," I gasped, my hand reaching for the door handle.

But before I could escape, Hank grabbed me with surprising strength and dragged me out of the truck, pulling me into the cabin.

"Why?" I managed to get out.

As we struggled, he whispered in my ear, "Revenge."

It all became clear now—he was seeking revenge for something I couldn't even fathom.

Terrified and helpless, I could only watch as Hank played out the twisted ending of the book, determined to exact his own form of justice by killing me. Every hit and blow of his fist intensified the pain shooting through my skull, and I could feel warm sticky blood seeping between my fingers as I grasped at my head.

"Hank, stop!" I pleaded, but his eyes were filled with a cold determination. "We can work this out," I gasped, fighting to catch my breath.

But Hank's grip on me only tightened as he sneered, "I don't want to hurt you, Morti, but sacrifices must be made in war." Before I could say anything else, his fist connected with my face, sending me into darkness.

Chapter Nineteen

As my eyes fluttered open, I found myself bound and shivering on a musty cot in a dilapidated cabin. The room was dimly lit by a single flickering bulb, casting eerie shadows along the walls. My body felt stiff and sore, but at least I was fully clothed—a small comfort in this terrifying situation. The sun peeked through the dirty window, offering little warmth to combat the chill that seeped into my bones.

I strained against my restraints, trying to assess how long I had been held captive in this desolate place. It seemed like days had passed since I had last seen the outside world. Suddenly, the sound of chopping wood echoed through the cabin, sending chills down my spine. It had to be Hank—the man who had brought me here against my will. My assistant ... someone I thought I could trust.

Panic set in, as I wondered why he hadn't killed me yet.

But then a glimmer of hope sparked within me. This might be my chance to escape. With trembling hands, I shuffled over to the broken window—a feeble attempt at insulation from the biting cold. My heart raced as I heard another swing of the ax outside. Timing it just right, I swung an old frying pan hanging above the stove towards the window, shattering it with a loud crash.

Before I could fully make my escape, something yanked me back into the room. It was Hank, grunting as he tossed me back onto the cot.

"Why haven't you killed me?" I gasped, wincing in pain from his rough handling.

"I decided it wouldn't be as satisfying without Collin here to watch." His words sent a chill down my spine.

"Who are you? Why do you hate him so much?"

"He took something precious away from me," Hank growled. "And now I want to do the same to him."

"But he doesn't love me," I protested.

"You're wrong about that," Hank sneered. "He just doesn't realize it yet."

"It doesn't matter. He's gone." I tried to convince myself as much as him.

"He'll be back," Hank assured me with a sinister smile.

"How do you know?"

"I sent word," he replied smugly.

"But you don't have his phone number."

"I don't need it. He'll see my message in *The King's Quills*," Hank boasted.

My mind raced trying to make sense of his words. "But I barely mentioned that group to you. I'm surprised you remember it."

"Hank Booker doesn't ... but Hans Brewmeister is all too familiar with it," he revealed, his true identity finally coming to light.

I couldn't believe it—the man who had terrorized me for days was someone else entirely. "You're Hans Brewmeister?" I gasped in shock.

"Yes. What better way for me to keep an eye on Oliver King?" He relished in my growing horror.

"I don't understand. Oliver King isn't in our group. It's meant for the fans."

"I've been waiting for years to get close enough to King to take my revenge," Hank explained with a twisted grin, ignoring my comment.

"But what does any of this have to do with Collin and me?"

"Don't you see, *Sybil*?" he taunted. "You are just a pawn in my game of revenge."

My heart sank as his words sunk in. "You know about that?" I asked, feeling exposed and vulnerable.

"I know everything," Hank gloated. "I hacked into Collin's IP account and read his private messages to you. When he mentioned meeting you in Mayflower, I knew this was my chance to finally get back at him, so I followed him."

"Wait, I thought you wanted revenge on Oliver King. What did Collin ever do to you?" I protested, desperately clinging to the last shred of hope.

"Tell yourself what you want to believe, but the truth is, Collin Quinn is Oliver King—the man who has been deceiving you all along," Hank revealed with a sinister smirk.

All the air whooshed out of my lungs, and I couldn't breathe. "No ... it can't be true," I managed to whisper in disbelief. "He's just a travel writer."

"Is that really so hard to believe?" Hank sneered. "You were the inspiration for his next thriller."

My stomach dropped as his words hit me like a ton of bricks. If what Hank said was true, then Collin didn't just lie about his identity. He'd used me. He could never have cared for me at all. I shook my head over and over as tears started trickling down my face.

"No one has ever seen the real Oliver King, so how can you be sure Collin is him?" I couldn't accept it—it was too much to bear.

"I've known him for decades, and we chose our pen names together," Hank declared triumphantly, then his expression hardened. "I never got to use mine."

"But he didn't recognize you?"

"Twenty years and a beard took care of that," he sneered.

My mind reeled as I tried to process everything. The man I had fallen in love with was nothing more than a fraud, using me for his own gain. And the other man I had come to know and trust as a friend had betrayed me. And now I was caught in the middle of a twisted game of revenge, unsure of whom to trust or where to turn.

Hank's voice trembled with rage and hurt as he continued, "He stole my dream and ruined my life, while he went on to make it big with *Veil of Secrets*. I knew it was him all along because of his pen name, a constant reminder of his betrayal." His fists clenched at his sides, knuckles turning white. "He disappeared soon after, never staying in one place long enough for me to find him." His eyes flashed with a burning intensity.

A bitter silence hung in the air before my question finally broke through. "Then why not just expose him to the world?"

Hank let out a bitter laugh, "Because that's not enough. I've been patiently waiting in *The King's Quills* for him to slip up so I could take something precious from him, something that would truly hurt him."

"Why me? Why didn't you kidnap the real Sybil?"

A twisted smile crossed Hank's face as he leaned in closer, his breath hot against my ear. "Because I've known for a long time that the online Sybil was the woman he was falling for. It took me a minute to figure out that you were her, so I waited until he came to his senses and got rid of the other one. I just didn't expect him to leave town before I had a chance to strike." Hank's expression twisted into a sinister grin.

My blood ran cold as I realized the danger I was in.

"Like I said, he won't be back." My voice was barely above a whisper, filled with fear and determination.

"And like I said, you're wrong about that."

ANOTHER COUPLE of days had passed, each one blurring into the next as I lay weak and helpless on the cot. Hank, my captor, was losing his grip on reality as he began to believe my words that Collin would not come looking for me. He had untied me but kept his distance, knowing that I was too sick to pose a threat.

The cabin we were in was old and rundown, with a broken window that let in the cold winter air. But Hank had taken care of us, boarding up the window and starting a fire in the stove. He even caught a rabbit for us to eat, all while anxiously waiting for his revenge on Collin after years of patience.

"I sent him coordinates," Hank muttered to himself as he paced back and forth in the small space. "He should have been here by now."

I swallowed nervously, afraid of what he might do if Collin didn't show up. "What are you going to do if he doesn't come?"

Hank's eyes gleamed with madness as they landed on me. "Follow through with the promise I sent him last night."

My heart pounded in fear as I asked, "And what was that?"

"That he had until one hour from now until I killed you." He checked his watch. "Tick-tock, Morti. It's up to him now."

Feeling desperate, I tried to reason with Hank. "I really need to use the bathroom."

He yanked me up roughly and dragged me to the bathroom. "Do your business quickly and don't try anything stupid."

As soon as the door closed behind him, I stood on the toilet and reached for the high window. It took some effort, but I managed to pry it open with its rusty hinges. My coat and shoes were still out in the living room where Hank had taken them from me. The snow had stopped falling, but there was still a thick layer on the ground. I knew I wouldn't make it far before freezing to death, but it was still better than being trapped with a crazed lunatic.

Taking a deep breath, I made my decision.

"Hurry up in there!"

"Almost done." I turned on the sink and hoped he couldn't hear the sound of the window squeaking open.

I had always wanted to be the hero of my own story, but why did my story have to be so much darker than my best friends'? I shook my head. That was just how things went for me. Without hesitation, I grabbed onto the windowsill and used all my strength to pull myself out and through the window. My arms scraped against the rough wood as I tumbled down into a snowbank, the impact cushioned by the thick snow.

Struggling to get back to my feet, I stumbled deeper

into the woods when suddenly the front door of the cabin burst open. "Time's up, Morti. Your clock just ran out." Hank's voice rang out behind me, followed by the sound of a rifle being cocked.

This was it. The end.

But then, something whizzed through the air, and someone pushed me to the ground. A deep voice yelled out just before a gunshot echoed through the trees. I was pinned under a body that felt all too familiar.

Collin Quinn.

Shouts and scuffling broke out in the background, but I could barely hear them over my racing heart. "Collin," I gasped. "I can't breathe. Can you move?"

No response.

"Please Collin, you're crushing me."

Still nothing.

Panic set in as I struggled to push him off me. Was he dead? But then I felt a pulse, and relief washed over me. He was alive, but injured. But if Collin was here ... then who was fighting with Hank, Hans, Hector—whoever he was?

My thoughts were interrupted as someone tried to pull me up and away from Collin's unconscious form. Suddenly, the reality of the situation hit me, and I knew that this was far from over.

My body ached as I scrambled to my feet, my eyes widening in recognition as three women and one man stood before me. My heart skipped a beat. It didn't matter that I had never seen them before ... I recognized them immediately. *The King's Quills*—a group of skilled and loyal allies. Savvy readers who had been on the case, pouring over clues and helping us figure out who our stalker was.

Tears filled my eyes and exhaustion made my body tremble.

"Oh, Morti, we're so glad to see you," one of the women, dressed in a beautiful rose-colored coat with a matching floral hat and scarf, exclaimed as she enveloped me in a tight hug.

Stacy Rose.

Normally I would have resisted, but this time I welcomed the comfort.

Another woman, young enough to be my daughter, rushed past us both in tactical gear and a backpack, tossing Stacy a thermal blanket she wrapped around me. The woman knelt beside Collin, expertly reviving him with smelling salts. "Stay with me, Quinn. Oliver King isn't going to die on my watch," she declared, her hands moving quickly as she bandaged his wound and tended to him. "I thought you'd be tougher than that."

That had to be She Wolf.

"Gideon Wolfe isn't real," Collin muttered weakly. "He's just a fictional character."

"Kind of like you," I couldn't help but interject.

Collin's eyes flew open and met mine. "Morti," he said weakly, "thank God you're okay. I don't know what I would have done if anything happened to you."

"Well, I'm no longer yours to worry about," I replied,

wrapping the blanket tighter around myself. "I'm not sure I ever was."

Dotty, or Tie Dye Dotty as she was known in the group, chimed in with a wink and her laid-back demeanor. "Oh now, you two can work it all out in the hospital. And lucky for you, I have all the medicine you need in my Scooby Doo van up by the road." Her long gray hair hung in waves over her tie-dyed coat, and her bell-bottom hems were caked with snow.

"How did you guys find me?" I asked in amazement.

"Ahoy there, Morti," Captain Rogers said with a salute, his captain's hat perched atop his head. "Hans put out a cryptic message to the group, but our clever lad Collin here deciphered it. Dotty drove, and I navigated the coordinates."

As I looked past them, I saw a man around my age jogging towards us with a lasso strapped to his hip. The tears finally fell as I realized I had survived. We were safe, and help was on its way.

Marky Mouse looked serious when he reached us out of breath. "Hans got away."

Deep down, I knew this wasn't the end of our troubles. As grateful as I was to be safe in the hands of my allies, something told me that we hadn't seen the last of our enemy, and my story wasn't over.

Chapter Twenty

The bitter chill of December had set in, signaling the arrival of Christmas. Dr. Joy had given me a thorough check-up after the incident, and Chaz had tended to Collin's wounds. While my physical bruises had healed, the emotional ones still lingered. Collin had tried to apologize and reconcile with me, but I couldn't bring myself to trust him again.

He had used me as his muse, nothing more.

And I was done playing his games.

I heard that he was out of the hospital and recovering from his gunshot wound. He tried to reach out to me numerous times, but I finally blocked him. Not only did he ruin our relationship, but he also tainted my love for Oliver King and *The Kings Quills*. The book club group had left for the holidays but promised to stay in touch.

"Here you go, MeMe." My father handed me a steaming mug of hot white chocolate.

I took a grateful sip and settled into a comfortable chair in front of Samantha's grand Christmas tree. Samantha and my father were both dressed in matching ugly light-up Christmas pajamas—she wore an elf hat, while he donned a Santa one. I, on the other hand, had opted for Casper-themed pajamas, but caved in and put on a pair of light-up reindeer antlers.

In previous years, my family would gather at my father's apartment to celebrate Christmas, but I couldn't bear to step foot in there without Collin by my side. My own apartment wasn't much better—everywhere I looked reminded me of him. So when they insisted that I stay with them in their new home during my recovery period, I was too exhausted to argue and gave in.

But if I were being honest, it was actually quite nice.

Samantha sat on the plush couch while my father played Santa Claus, handing out presents like he did every year since I was born. As I watched them interact, it was clear to see the love between them—my father had finally beaten cancer and was off his hormones, giving him a second chance at happiness. He deserved it, after everything he went through with my mother.

And with me.

I wasn't an easy child to raise, and even now, I still had my moments. But after surviving being kidnapped and given a second chance at life, I promised myself to do better and not let my fears hold me back.

"Okay my favorite girls, time to open your presents." My father beamed with pride.

I thanked both him and Samantha for their thoughtful gifts of all my favorite things, but when I came across the last one, I blinked in disbelief. It was a contract signing over the family business to me.

I looked up at my father with tears in my eyes, "Are you sure?"

"I'm positive. You've earned it, honey. I'm so proud of you."

I swallowed the lump in my throat and gave him a tight hug. "Thank you, Dad. I won't let you down."

"I know you won't." He winked before turning to Samantha. "Your turn now."

Samantha squealed with excitement as she unwrapped gift after gift from my father. Even though I had bought her a sultry negligee to make up for not participating in her shower raffle, I couldn't bear to look over at the expression on my father's face as she opened it. But her eyes lit up when she received her final gift from him—a set of sparkling diamond earrings and matching tennis bracelet that complemented her engagement ring perfectly.

"These are perfect! I love them so much!" She threw herself into my father's arms. "I love you so much, my Pooh Bear. You spoil me."

"And I will continue to do so because you deserve it, my darling." My father kissed her lovingly.

"Your turn, Dad." I smiled as he tore into his gifts like a child, oohing and aahing over each one.

"Now open your special gift from me!" Samantha

clapped her hands excitedly. "It will go perfectly with Morti's gift to me."

I raised an eyebrow in curiosity, prepared to look away if necessary.

My father opened a long, slender box wrapped in a luxurious satin ribbon. His eyes widened in surprise as he looked down at the contents in his hands. Slowly, he raised his gaze to meet hers. "These are plane tickets."

With a grin, she nodded. "That's right. Two tickets to paradise. We're going to Hawaii!"

He furrowed his brow in confusion. "For our honeymoon? But these are for two days from now. Our wedding isn't until another week on New Year's Day. I thought we were going to wait until spring for our honeymoon cruise."

Her smile only grew wider. "Oh, but spring is no good because this isn't just a honeymoon." She bounced on her toes with excitement. "It's a babymoon! And I've decided I want us to elope."

"What?" Both my father and I exclaimed in unison, our mouths hanging open in shock.

All that work ... the wedding was fully planned, booked, and supplied. I shook my head in disbelief and bit back a sigh.

My father's face paled.

She clapped her hands together happily. "I'm pregnant! Isn't it wonderful?" She patted my father's hand. "It'll be okay, Mortimer. I'm young and healthy ... and not *her*."

And I was in shock. My jaw fell open. I couldn't be more surprised if I tried.

Tears glistened in my father's eyes as he smiled at her. "I can't say I'm not terrified, but that's the best Christmas gift of all."

"Speaking of surprises ..." My heart fluttered with anticipation as I spoke up, wanting to join in on the excitement. "I guess that means you'll love my gift as well," I said, catching their attention. "Because I'm pregnant, too."

AFTER MANY TEARS of joy and fear, we were all coming to terms with what our new family would look like. Two days had passed, and now I found myself seated at a cozy table in *Pilgrim Perks Cafe* with my best friends—Zoe, Tiffany, and Harmony. The aroma of freshly brewed coffee and warm pastries permeated the air.

"Did you hear the news? Sylvia Stallone finished her book—an erotic thriller about an adult entertainer on the run—and it's being published." I shook my head in amazement. "Sybil Starr is no more, but her social media fans launched Sylvia Stallone straight onto the bestseller's list. Who knew?"

"Good for her, and good riddance." Harmony shrugged. "Maybe it will keep her out of Mayflower for good this time."

"Forget Sybil," Tiffany said as she stirred sugar into her

tea. "I still can't wrap my head around the fact that your dad and Samantha eloped and are on their way to Hawaii as we speak."

"And to think she's pregnant," Zoe added, sprinkling cinnamon onto her latte.

"Speaking of pregnancies, Morticia, when are you going to tell Collin?" Harmony asked, sipping her black coffee.

"I don't even know where he is," I replied with a shrug, memories of my traumatic kidnapping and beating flooding back to me. "No address, remember?"

Just then, the barista approached our table carrying a large package. "Morticia Smith?" she asked.

"Yes," I answered cautiously.

"This is for you," she said as she handed me the package. She then pointed to the TV that had just switched from commercials to a daytime talk show. "And you're supposed to watch this right now."

Confused, we turned our attention to the TV hanging on the wall and gasped in unison.

Collin Quinn.

"I thought he didn't do interviews," Harmony said with surprise.

"Oliver King doesn't," I clarified, ripping open the package and pulling out a book. I stared at the cover in disbelief.

"Collin Quinn?" Tiffany exclaimed as she took the book from my hands.

I nodded, my jaw dropping in shock. "I'm not sure what game he's playing now, but he's not using Oliver King as a pen name anymore."

"Maybe he's not playing a game," Zoe offered gently. "And that doesn't look like a thriller to me."

The cover depicted *Smith's Funeral Home* with Freedom Lake as its backdrop, and a lone woman who bore an uncanny resemblance to me stood on the front porch.

As we watched, the host of the talk show asked Collin, "So tell me, what made you venture away from thrillers to write *Shadows and Light?*"

Collin sat there looking handsome and confident and ... alive. My heart ached at the sight of him. "It was time," he replied into the microphone. "I was in a dark place for a long time, but then I met someone. A woman who changed everything for me. She brought light into my shadowed world, and I haven't been the same since."

"But the book ends so sad," the host pointed out.

"That's true. I never was any good at writing romance," Collin acknowledged. "I'll try not to give too many spoilers away. The man made mistakes and regrets them deeply, but they can't be undone. He has to live with the consequences of his actions. Find the courage to stop hiding and truly live again."

"Is that why you're not using your pen name, Oliver King? Why you came out of hiding and revealed your true identity?"

"Oliver King is a part of my past—a significant part

that I don't regret because it led me to where I am today. But now, it's time to move on." Collin looked directly into the camera, his gaze piercing through my heart. "I'm done running and hiding. It's time I fought for what I truly want instead of what's expected of me."

"Like writing in this genre? Is this book part of a series? Can we expect a sequel?" the host prodded.

"That remains to be seen," Collin answered with a small smile. "But I have hope that this new character will be rewarded for his changed ways."

"In other words, you hope he gets the girl in the end?"

"Isn't that what we all want? Love? Love would be the greatest gift of all."

"There you have it, folks," the host announced. "A brand-new story you won't want to miss, out in stores on New Year's Day by the new and improved Collin Quinn."

With trembling hands, I flipped open the cover of the book to reveal the dedication page. A lump formed in my throat as tears filled my eyes, blurring the words on the page. The dedication read:

To Morti,

For the woman who changed everything ... I was a fool. I love you with all my heart and will spend the rest of my life making it up to you if you'll let me.

Forever yours, Collin.

Zoe's soft voice broke through my thoughts, her own tears falling as she asked, "What are you going to do?"

"You know we're here for you, whatever you decide,"

Tiffany added, sniffling and dabbing a tissue under her eyes.

"Ditto." Harmony cleared her throat and blew her nose.

My heart ached as I replied, "What can I do? I don't know where he is," I said.

"But I know where you are." A deep familiar voice spoke from behind me, and I turned around in shock as my heart exploded at the sight of him. There stood Collin, his arms open wide, and his eyes filled with hope for everyone to see.

Without hesitation, I threw myself into his embrace, feeling the warmth and safety of his arms wrapped around me. "The answer is yes," I whispered.

"What's the question?" he chuckled softly.

"The question you meant to ask me, of course," I said louder. "Yes, I'll marry you, so you can spend your life making it up to me." I winked at the girls gaping at me, then looked my fiancé in the eyes. "You're not the only one who has changed and is ready to go after what she wants. By the way, it turns out you're my baby daddy after all. I'm rather partial of your old genes. Congratulations."

"I'm going to be a father?" A slow smile spread across Collin's face, his eyes filling with love and wonder.

"You are," I confirmed with a smile of my own. "Now what do you say we rewrite the ending of your book? I told you we would make a great team."

"I say you've got a deal. You are the most interesting

woman I've ever met, Morticia Smith. I love you. Let's do this thing."

"I love you, too. How does January First sound? I have the most amazing spot, and it's already planned, just waiting for a bride and groom."

"It's a date," he said softly before sealing our agreement with a kiss full of promise and hope for our very own happily-ever-after.

Epilogue

January First dawned with the promise of a sunny and bright day. It was finally my wedding day. The anticipation and excitement bubbling within me were almost palpable, but there was also a hint of nervousness lingering in the back of my mind.

What could possibly go wrong ...

Despite it being winter, Samantha had always dreamed of having an outdoor wedding. My father had different ideas—he wanted to keep the wedding small and have it at the one place that meant the most to him ... *Smith's Funeral Home.*

However, now that he and Samantha had eloped and flown off to their honey-baby-moon in Hawaii, I couldn't bear the thought of letting all the time and money we spent on planning this event go to waste. And with my own pregnancy a factor, time was of the essence, so I never cancelled anything.

I had convinced my father not to come home, wanting Samantha and him to fully enjoy their trip. In return, I promised that we would celebrate both our weddings when they returned. In a bold move, I had decided to wear my mother's wedding dress, despite my fears of turning out just like her.

I had learned to let go of those fears and accept that she had turned her life around when she became pregnant with me. She'd just had too many underlying health issues from years of abusing her body, and it had taken her in childbirth. She had loved me unconditionally, just as I loved my unborn child ... and her.

"You look breathtaking, hon," Zoe said, giving me a hug.

"I'm so happy all your dreams are coming true, doll." Tiffany squeezed my hand with tears in her eyes. "You deserve this."

"They're right, babe." Harmony nodded. "No one deserves their happily-ever-after more than you. The fourth musketeer's finale. I'm so happy for us all."

"Me too." I blinked back my own tears. "You know you'll all be my first loves, right?"

They nodded, and the four of us gave a group hug and said a little cheer, renewing our vow to still be there for all our second acts.

Inhaling a deep breath, I looked around as my girls took their places.

The beauty of the pristine white snow covering the ground glistened in the sunlight reflecting off the lake where our ceremony was taking place. A large tent with multiple heaters scattered about was set up for warmth. In attendance were Father O'Dority and Sister Mary Agness, along with our close friends and family.

Captain Rogers, assisted by Tie Dye Dotty, was chosen to officiate our ceremony. My dear friend Stacy Rose stood by my side as my maid of honor—the rose to my thorn— because I couldn't choose among my best friends—my soul sisters. So, Zoe, Tiffany, and Harmony were my brides- maids. Collin had chosen his best man and protege She Wolf, and his new friends Chaz, Matt, and Bryon as his groomsmen. Even Marky Mouse had a special role as the ring bearer.

As we made our way to the start of the aisle, lit with candles by Clyde and decorated with flowers by Beatrice, our closest friends played their parts in the ceremony— Eddy and Annette scattering rose petals along the red satin runway, and Eli decorating Fester with "Just Married" paraphernalia and an "Until Death" sign. But before our grand adventure as newlyweds could begin, our friends walked down the aisle together to take their places on either side of the altar.

Suddenly, the 'mysterious and spooky and altogether ooky' music began to play, and everyone stood to turn around and look at me. I sucked in a little breath, realizing I was the center of attention, but then I caught sight of Collin at the altar. In that moment, any fears or anxieties melted away. I knew I was exactly where I was meant to be, and everything was going to be okay.

Truman Winters held out his arm and smiled at me. "You ready?"

I nodded. "Yes," I said, and meant it.

Truman proudly escorted me down the aisle and handed me off to Gertrude who stood in for my father.

"Who gives this lovely landlubber away?" Captain Rogers asked.

"Her father, and well, I—in his place—do." Tears glistened in her eyes as she dabbed at them with a handkerchief and planted a kiss on my cheek before taking her seat.

I stepped forward to stand beside Collin at the altar, his stormy gray eyes now soft and misty with emotion.

"You look absolutely stunning," he whispered, his voice full of emotion and the storm clouds in his eyes a soft foggy mist.

"And you look incredibly handsome," I replied, feeling my heart swell with love for him.

Captain Rogers cleared his throat and began the ceremony, his booming voice carrying through the crisp winter air. "Ahoy there, dearly beloved," he began. "We are gathered here today to witness the union of landlubbers Morticia Smith and Collin Quinn. In a world where love can feel as fleeting as the snowflakes falling around us, it is rare to find a bond that shines brightly against the chill of life's uncertainties."

As he spoke, I felt the warmth of Collin's warm hand envelope mine, grounding me in this sea of emotions. I looked around at our friends, their presence serving as my anchor in this moment.

"Today marks not just a moment but a journey—a journey forged in vulnerability, commitment, and change," Captain Rogers continued. "Morticia and Collin have chosen to face their future together, embracing both the light and the dark on the horizon."

"Peace and love to you both as you sail through this journey of life," Tie Dye Dotty added with a playful wink.

Then came the familiar words, "Do you, Collin, take Morticia—sometimes known as Sybil—to be your lawfully wedded mate, to have and to hold, from this day forward, for better, for worse, for richer, for poorer, in sickness and in health, to love and to cherish, until death do you part for Davey Jones locker?"

"I do," Collin replied, his voice filled with warmth and conviction.

"And do you, Morticia, take Collin—sometimes known as Oliver—to be your lawfully wedded mate, to have and to hold, from this day forward, for better, for worse, for richer, for poorer, in sickness and in health, to love and to cherish, until death do you part for Davey Jones locker?"

"I do," I said without hesitation.

"Then by the power vested in me by the laws of the sea and the authority granted to me as captain of this ceremony, I now pronounce you husband and wife. You may kiss the bride."

"We did it, my love," Collin whispered, as he bent down and pressed his lips to mine.

Suddenly, just like in my dream that felt like a lifetime ago, I heard a loud engine roaring in the distance. Only, this time it wasn't a train ... it was Hans Brewmeister behind the wheel of a craft beer tractor trailer, crashing through the bushes into the backyard and heading straight for us.

Everyone started screaming and running out of the way.

But before he could reach us and ruin everything once and for all, Eli appeared from out of nowhere driving the funeral home's newest hearse. He collided with the truck, throwing it off course and causing it to crash into Freedom Lake.

People were shouting, trying to find a way to help, when Hans emerged from the wreckage brandishing a gun. More gasps and chaos ensued, but Marky Mouse swooped in with his lasso out, roping Hans's arm just in time to prevent a tragedy.

In a matter of minutes, Officer Pickles, who happened to be in attendance of our wedding, had Hans handcuffed and placed in the back of his patrol car. Eli emerged from the hearse without a scratch to cheers from everyone.

As I held onto Collin tightly, my heart was racing from the unexpected turn of events until the shock finally wore off. "That was a plot twist I never saw coming," I finally said, "but I'm glad that Hans is out of the picture for good. Now nothing can come between you and me as husband and wife and our happily-ever-after."

"Ahh, yes, now *that's* a rewrite I don't mind one bit." And then my husband pressed his lips to mine, making all my dreams come true.

Books By Kari Lee Townsend

KALLI BALLAS MYSTERY

Mind Over Murder

Two Cents of Doom

A Touch of Malice

An Inkling of Evil

Mayhem on the Mind

CECE MONROE MYSTERY

Harmful Habits

SUNNY MEADOWS MYSTERY

Tempest in the Tea Leaves

Corpse in the Crystal Ball

Trouble in the Tarot

Shenanigans in the Shadows

Perish in the Palm

Hazard in the Horoscope

Chaos and Cold Feet

Murder in the Meditation

Cruising into Danger

Road Trip to Ruin

DIGITAL DIVA

Talk to the Hand

Rise of the Phenoteens

Books By Kari Lee Harmon

COLDWATER COVE

Dark Seas

Frozen Waters

Dangerous Thaw

Deadly Frost

STANDALONE NOVELS

Valley of Secrets

Until Tomorrow

Project Produce

Love Lessons

LAKEHOUSE TREASURES NOVELLAS

James

Amber

Meghan

Brook

MERRY SCROOG-MAS NOVELLAS

Naughty or Nice

Sleigh Bells Ring

Jingle all the Way

About the Author

Kari Lee Townsend is a National Bestselling Author of mysteries & a tween superhero series. She also writes romance and women's fiction as Kari Lee Harmon. With a background in English education, she's now a full-time writer, wife to her own superhero, mom of 3 sons, 1 darling diva, 1 daughter-in-law & 3 lovable fur babies. These days you'll find her walking her dogs or hard at work on her next story, living a blessed life.